Praise for the Destination: Desire series

"I loved this amazing, emotional love story... A tear or two became commonplace during some intense scenes. In Ms. Jordan's talented hands, the characters evolved naturally and realistically, flaws and all."
-Harlequin Junkie Reviews

"5 stars. My favorite in the series so far. I just loved the back story of this couple and it's just a different twist on a romance. Loved it!" *-Kristi Simonsen*

"This is an well written story, where you get invested in the characters and root for them to have their HEA...I cannot wait to see what comes next in this series. 5 stars" *-Gigi Staub*

"This was a fabulous story with great characters... one of the best I've read this year. I LOVED this." *-Jennifer McKenzie*

Never Let GO

DESTINATION: DESIRE
BOOK 2

C. JORDAN

CJ BOOKS

contents

Dedication

This one is for the Professor Moriarty, who took me to Hawaii for Christmas and bought me Hong Kong buns and pineapple floats. Without you, this book would never have been written.

And for my librarian colleague who shall not be named to protect his innocence—thanks for recommending we check out Olomana on that island holiday trip. Great music!

CHAPTER ONE

Half Moon Bay, California

"Julie?" Karen called from the front of the shop. "Julie, where are you?"

"In the back." A bittersweet sensation swamped Julie as she gazed around Purl Moon Fiber Arts. Wooden shelves held stacks of every imaginable color and fiber of yarn—a beautiful, touchable rainbow. An old-fashioned spinning wheel dominated one corner, and the basket beside it contained a long braid of roving wool just waiting to be spun. It was the last batch of wool she'd hand-died with her great-aunt. She hadn't been able to make herself finish it.

Tears stung her eyes, but a smile curled her lips. Damn, she missed Auntie Eloise. The feisty old woman had taught Julie to knit and crochet in this very shop. She'd learned to spin on that wheel. Lovely memories.

"Here you are." Karen came around one of the display shelves. "Are you ready?"

Reaching over, Julie unplugged the lights on the miniature Christmas tree. Crocheted snowflake decorations graced every branch, most of them Auntie's creations. Putting up the tree had always been something Julie and Eloise did together, but this year she was on her own. It was too much, too painful. She'd held it together during the worst of the holiday shopping rush, but it was four days before Christmas and she was closing up and getting out of town. She just couldn't bear it.

Clearing her throat, she turned to her friend. "Ready as I'll ever be. Is Tate with you?"

Karen's face fell a little before she pasted on a wide grin. "He couldn't make it, but he said to tell you happy holidays and have fun. He's busy with work today."

And every other day, but Julie didn't say it. Things weren't golden in Karen's marriage, which was a shame. Julie liked Tate, always had, but he was a workaholic who wasn't giving his wife what she needed. If things didn't improve soon, she wasn't sure what would happen, but the shadows in Karen's eyes said she was reaching the end of her tolerance.

Stepping forward, Julie gave her friend a hug. They both could use one right now. It had been a rough year. "Hang in there, sweetie."

Karen squeezed her tight. "You too."

The bell jangled over the shop door. Anne shouted, "Are you two about done? Meg's out here worrying about Julie missing her flight! You know how I hate listening to Meg nag. Get a move on!"

"I'm coming, I'm coming!" Julie rolled her eyes and let Karen go. She pointed to a big suitcase, her purse propped on top. "Grab my bags, will you?"

"Sure."

A quick check of Purl Moon showed the windows and doors were closed and locked. She switched off the lights, set the security system, and motioned Karen ahead of her. Once they'd exited, she secured the deadbolt on the front door.

Cool air wrapped around her, the salty hint of the Pacific Ocean curling into her nose. Tidy little shops like hers ran up and down Main Street, looking like a scene from a postcard, all festooned with Christmas lights and wreaths to celebrate the season. A season Julie wanted to escape.

"It's about time you got out of town," Anne barked. "You need a vacation."

"Well, what do you think the baggage is for?" Julie winked at her friend, who stuck out her tongue in return.

Julie watched Anne wrestle the enormous suitcase she was taking to Hawaii into the back of a subcompact car. She wasn't sure how the other woman managed that feat of engineering, but she wasn't about to question it either. Anne was tall, wiry, athletic, and as sarcastic as she was opinionated. Even luggage and the laws of physics bowed before her tenacity.

The four of them—Meg, Julie, Anne, and Karen—had been a tight-knit group since elementary school. Julie was grateful for their friendship, but never more so than the last year. They'd been a solid support as Julie watched her great-aunt's health fade. They'd all been there in the hospital with her when Auntie Eloise had passed.

Hot grief poured through Julie, making her clench her fists at her sides. It wasn't fair. Eloise had still been so *alive*, so active. She'd run her own business right up until she'd had a series of small strokes that had left her struggling to walk and speak clearly. Julie had been living in San Francisco at the time, working as an office manager, but she'd come back to help out, taking over Purl Moon until the spunky old lady could get back on her feet.

It had never happened.

Two months later, a massive stroke had stolen Auntie Eloise's life. Over. Done. Gone. Just that quickly. Julie tried to tell herself that Eloise had lived a long, full life, that she'd had a lot of years to do all the things she enjoyed. But it didn't help much. It still just *hurt*.

"I'm really glad you're getting a break. You need it, honey." Meg walked up with a carrying container filled with two cups of coffee from a café across the street. She glanced at Karen. "Finn's saving us a table for when we finally get rid of these girls."

"Oh, *loverboy*," Anne sang out. "I hooked you guys up, don't forget it. You'd still be giving him a case of blue balls if it weren't for me."

Julie had to bite her lip to keep from chortling like an immature teenager. Karen rocked back on her heels, her green eyes dancing with mirth.

"How could anyone forget your act of daring in convincing me to have a wild week in Vegas? My hero. I'll have Finn start writing thank you cards every time he gets some. Just to show how happy he is to be less blue." Meg sighed dramatically before she handed the liquid ambrosia to Julie, then popped open the passenger door of Anne's car to set the remaining cup in the console. When she straightened and their eyes met, there was enough sympathy in her friend's gaze to make Julie's throat tighten, and any urge to laugh died away. Meg said softly, "It'll be good for you to have some time to yourself."

"You should hook up with a nice Hawaiian cabana boy. Get him to teach you the hula...in bed." Anne slammed the trunk closed and did a bad imitation of the hula, with a less than subtle bump-and-grind move thrown in.

"Oh Jesus. Don't ever do that in public again." Karen shook her head. "And you teach impressionable children."

"It is amazing they let me loose around kids, isn't it?" Anne ruffled a hand over her shock of red hair.

Julie tightened the belt on her coat and gave Meg a look. "Are you sure you and Finn want to do Christmas with her?"

"Her, her three whacky sisters, and her drama mama, you mean?" Meg waggled her eyebrows and brushed an unruly curl away from her face. The cold, misting winter rain did nothing to help her tame her hair. "We'll survive. Probably."

Julie wrapped each of her friends in a quick hug before sliding into the car. Karen held the door for her and shut it after Julie drew her legs in. She heard Karen's muffled voice through the glass. "Okay, Anne. Try not to kill anyone on the way to the airport. Auto accidents make for bad vacation starters."

Bouncing into the driver's seat, Anne pushed the button to roll down the passenger window and leaned across Julie to blow a raspberry at Meg and Karen. "For the record, I am a fantastic driver, and my family is *awesome* during the holidays. We put the fun in dysfunctional."

The four of them burst into giggles before Anne gunned her little car down Main Street. It felt good to laugh. Julie hadn't done enough of it lately. Anne had offered to have Julie over for the dysfunctional fun, but she needed to get out of Half Moon Bay. She needed to get away from anything that reminded her of Aunt Eloise. Honolulu was just the ticket. A week of lounging on the beach sipping cocktails sounded like heaven right now. No worries, no stress. A little grin tugged at her mouth. Who knew? Maybe she'd even find some nice cabana boy to teach her the hula...in bed.

CHAPTER TWO

I t was official. She was lost.

Julie's sense of direction had never been great, but Waikiki Beach wasn't all that big, so she should have been fine. She executed a slow pirouette, trying to see if she recognized any landmarks or street signs. Nope. Nothing.

"Awesome." She snorted at herself. Ah, well. She was on vacation, right? There was no hurry.

She'd forgotten to bring a pair of nice shoes to go with the fancy dress she'd brought for Christmas dinner. She'd made reservations at the Royal Hawaiian, and showing up in sequins and flipflops would just be tacky, so she'd found her way to the nearby mall and scored a fantastic deal on some strappy heels. The excitement had lasted until she realized that she'd exited the large shopping center in a different place than she'd entered. And now she wasn't entirely certain where she was—the map on her cell phone just confused her—and though it was blissfully warm, the sky was starting to take on an ominous shade of gray. This was not a good sign.

Glancing up, she saw a massive metal and glass building with a sign that said *Hawaii Convention Center*. "Perfect."

Forget trying to find her way back. A convention center had to be an easy place to catch a cab. She jogged across the street just as the clouds opened up and rain pelted down on her. Laughing, she shot forward to make it under the overhang, only slightly soaked. She shook the water droplets out of her hair and then headed toward a crowd of people milling near the entrance. The front curb teemed with taxis, buses, and airport shuttles. It looked like some kind of event had just let out. Not great, but she'd live.

A few minutes later, she found someone who looked like they worked there. "Hi, I need to get to the Hilton Hawaiian Village. Which one is the cab line?"

"Would you care to share my taxi?" a deep voice called from behind her. "We're going to the same place, it seems."

Turning, she saw a tall man holding open the door to a cab. He was...sexy. Dark hair, serious blue eyes, angular features that contrasted with a sensual mouth. She took a few steps forward, her feet moving without any direction from her brain. Seriously, anyone that good to look at deserved a closer inspection. She had to tilt her head back to meet his gaze by the time she stopped. And he looked even better from this angle. Something about him made her heart skip a beat.

He leaned toward her, closing some of the distance between them. She didn't back away. Somehow, it felt just right to have him in her personal space. His eyes crinkled at the corners, though he didn't smile. "Should I take your coming over as a yes?"

"Yes." The word came out throatier and more inviting than she meant it to.

His gaze dropped for just a moment to where her damp T-shirt clung to her breasts, and her breath caught, a shiver of utterly sexual awareness passing through her. Her nipples tightened. She wanted to tell herself it was from the breeze on her wet clothes, but it would have been a lie. Her reaction to this man was hot, instantaneous—a lightning strike of sheer need.

Mmm-hmm. She could only hope she wasn't drooling. A flush burned her cheeks. Wow, she hadn't realized she was this hard up. Okay, so it *had* been a while since she'd let herself enjoy the company of a man. Not since before Auntie's first stroke. She lifted her chin. It was time to get on with living her life, even if it would always be a little bit emptier without Eloise.

Tilting her head, Julie looked the dark-haired man over one more time. Maybe not the most gorgeous guy she'd ever seen, but definitely the sexiest she'd been around in a long time. Hello, animal magnetism. She knew her attraction showed in her expression, but she couldn't bring herself to care. The tingle of warmth spreading through her felt pretty good.

She cleared her throat, recognizing that she'd been staring a little too long. "Thanks for sharing your ride."

"No problem." His gaze did a slow slide down her body, the perusal deliberate and as obvious as her inspection of him had been.

Her shoulder brushed over his chest as she bent to climb into the car. Just that simple touch made her shudder, and a wave of sweet heat sluiced through her. Holy Jesus, this was crazy. She had no idea who he was, but she hoped he was single. It would be a damn shame to be this drawn to a guy who was taken. She dragged in a deep breath and realized that her heart had leaped into a pounding rush.

Sliding across the seat, she set her shopping bag on the floor at her feet. He climbed in after her, dropping a leather messenger bag on the seat between them. He leaned his head back against the seat, closed his eyes, and sighed. The cab pulled away from the curb and merged into the chaotic mess of people trying to get out of the rain and into some form of transportation.

Julie twisted in her seat to get a better look at her companion. Yes, definitely gorgeous. And definitely exhausted. "Long day?"

Rolling his head toward her, he opened his eyes. He offered her a slight grin. "Oh, yeah. I just finished a week-long conference, but now I'm free to relax, unwind, and...enjoy myself."

The faintest hint of an accent flavored his words, but she couldn't pinpoint where he might be from. A mystery. She liked that. But then what he'd said sank in.

"You finished? So you're on your way home?" A pang of disappointment went through her. She shouldn't care, but she did. The possibility shimmering between them was too good to miss out on so easily.

Two dimples popped into his cheeks. "Not at all. I'm staying for another week on vacation."

Now that sounded more promising. "At the Hilton?"

"Yes, and you?" His gaze sharpened with interest, and another shiver of awareness went through her. She hadn't been this intensely attracted to a man in forever, and it was even headier than she remembered.

She tucked a lock of hair behind her ear. "I'm staying there too, until after Christmas. I flew in this morning."

"Oh, yeah? Where are you from?" He shifted his shoulders against the seat, turning a little to face her. His scent drifted to her—musky male and a light, spicy cologne. He swallowed, and she watched his Adam's apple bob. A totally inappropriate desire to lean over and slide her tongue along the strong column of his throat hit her.

He stared at her, one eyebrow arched. Ah, yes. He'd asked her a question. *Get it together, Julie.*

"California. Just outside of San Francisco." She held out her hand to shake, because she *had* to know what it was like to feel his skin against hers. "I'm Julie, by the way. Julie Simms."

His gaze drifted from her hand to her face, and the look in his eyes told her the attraction was definitely *not* one-sided. He didn't ogle her, but his interest was clear. "Lukas Klein. I'm a physics professor, and you?"

"I run a fiber arts store." When he took her hand, she felt the restrained power in his grip. His palm had slight calluses that rasped against her flesh, and a flash of need sparked within her. Nice. Now that was what she called chemistry.

The cab swayed as it took a turn, and Julie caught a glimpse of the bronze hula dancer sculptures that signaled the entrance to the Hilton Hawaiian Village. Not much time before she had to say goodbye to this man. And she didn't want to. She was drawn to him, she was curious enough about him to want to know more, and she was free to pursue something if she dared.

And she noticed he hadn't let her hand go yet. In fact, he skimmed his thumb across the inside of her wrist. Goose bumps erupted over her skin, and her nipples beaded to thrust against her bra.

"May I ask you something?" He pitched his voice low enough that their driver wouldn't be able to hear him.

She nodded. "Yes."

"Are you in Honolulu alone?" He held up his free hand to stop her from answering. "No, that's not what I want to ask. Are you married or otherwise engaged?"

"Totally single." And available for whatever he'd had in mind when he asked that question. Insane? Maybe. But if she couldn't do something a little wild on her vacation, when could she?

His grip tightened on her hand. "Me too."

"Are you free for a drink tonight, Lukas?" The words were out of her mouth before she gave them any real thought, but she didn't wish to call the question back.

"Yes, I am." His smile was slow and hot enough to burn, and an answering fire kindled inside of her. He swept his thumb over her palm. "How does meeting at nine o'clock in the Tapa Bar sound to you? It's in the hotel."

"Perfect," she replied. Better than perfect. It felt like she was coming back to the land of the living. Just what she needed on this trip. For the first time in forever, she was *really* looking forward to something.

E xhaustion warred with anticipation inside of Lukas. It had since the moment he'd left Julie in the hotel lobby. Sighing, he propped his shoulder against the tall window that flanked the sliding glass door in his room. From there, he could take in the sweep of beach and ocean that spread before him.

The week had been a long one, with a conference that required non-stop energy and focus while he met with well-known scholars in his field. It was always mentally stimulating, but draining since the days could last well into the nights as they discussed and debated various physics topics. He'd intended to crash in his room for the night, but meeting Julie had thrown a wrench into those plans. Feeling her lush curves slide against him when she'd stepped out of the cab had left him too wired to sleep. The contact had been brief, but more than enough to send adrenaline and lust rushing through his veins. An ironic grin touched his lips at how his body had betrayed him. Nope, there was no way he'd sleep until after their drink tonight.

Maybe not then, either, if he were lucky. A man had to have his priorities.

His stomach rumbled, reminding him that he'd been running on caffeine most of the day. Tilting his wrist, he checked his watch. He'd made dinner reservations at one of the hotel restaurants that morning, knowing he'd be tired and unwilling to go far for food. As the day ground to a close and he just wanted to collapse in bed, he'd made a mental note to cancel the reservation. Good thing he hadn't gotten around to it.

Pushing away from window, he patted his pockets to check that he had his wallet and room key. It only took a few minutes for the elevator to get him to the ground level, and he strolled through the open-air hotel. The scent of the ocean filled his nostrils, and he could just hear the crashing of waves over the sound of gleeful children squealing and splashing in the water. Strolling down paths that were lined with koi ponds, he made his way to the Rainbow Lanai restaurant. He loved the rounded alcoves that belled toward the beach. There were no windows to block the sea breeze—everything here was open.

He paused for a moment to take in the beach and let the sounds of the ocean relax him after the work-intensive week. After turning to walk toward the restaurant entrance, he drew up short when he saw Julie standing there. Like a magnet, he was drawn to her.

The hostess gave her an apologetic glance. "I'm sorry, ma'am. We only do reservations during the holidays, but without one, the wait will be over an hour."

"Oh." The reply was disgruntled, and Julie wrinkled her nose. "There goes that idea. Can you recommend anywhere else I could—"

Lukas didn't bother resisting the urge to reach for her. He wanted to feel that buzz of attraction again. She jolted when he set his hand on her shoulder, her dark eyes darting back to see who touched her. He liked the way her breathing hitched when she realized it was him. Very nice. Slipping his palm down her side to settle at her hip, he addressed the hostess. "I have a reservation under Klein. I assume if my party goes from one to two, that won't be too much of a problem, will it?"

"No, Mr. Klein. That's just fine." The woman checked his name off a list. "If you'll both come with me, please?"

Julie gave him a dazzling smile. "You seem to have a knack for coming to my rescue, Lukas."

"My pleasure." He pressed his hand to the small of her back to urge her forward.

Damn, she was lovely. Not beautiful in an overblown kind of way, but she definitely made him look twice. The memory of the first time he'd seen her still struck him. Running across the street to get out of the rain, her eyes alight with laughter, her wet clothing clinging to her curves. His body had tightened with visceral want, making him throw out his usual reserve and invite her to share his cab. Seeing her now only intensified those feelings.

"What can I get you to drink?" the hostess asked as she motioned them to a table that lined one of the alcoves.

"Oh, what a view!" Delight shone in Julie's gaze as she took in the ocean scene before them.

Lukas grinned at her enthusiasm. He felt the same way every time he dined here. Clearing his throat, he glanced at the hostess. "I'll have an iced tea."

"Anything you like, Mr. Klein." She gave him a flirtatious glance, but he found himself unmoved. He was already too intrigued by Julie to be distracted.

Julie apparently caught the exchange and arched her eyebrows at the other woman. "It's *Dr.* Klein, actually. He's a physics professor. And I'll have lemonade, thanks."

Clearing dismissed, the hostess flounced off and Lukas coughed into his fist, trying not to snicker. Julie leaned closer, letting her hair fall forward to cover her face. "It *is* Dr. Klein, isn't it? Professors have doctorates, right?"

"Yes, I have a doctorate, though not all professors do." He chuckled, lifting his hand to brush a dark lock behind her ear. The silky feel of her hair sliding against his skin made him wish they were in a far more intimate setting, especially when she swayed toward him, her lips parting in silent invitation. "You are incredibly attractive, Ms. Simms."

She flushed, opening her mouth to respond, but the hostess returned with their drinks and broke the moment. A shame. He'd have loved to hear what her reply would have been, and if it would have been flustered or tempting. He wasn't sure which would be more provocative.

After the hostess left again, Lukas spread his hands. "Shall we sit for a moment or go straight for the buffet?"

"Dive into the food, of course. I'm starving and this place is supposed to be good."

"It is." He gestured for her to precede him, and he enjoyed the sway of her hips as she walked toward the first food station. She had an amazing ass, one he'd like to get his hands on. There was no telling yet if this attraction would lead them to the bedroom, but a man could hope. He sighed in appreciation when she bent forward a bit to scoot around a table packed with people and her skirt tightened over her backside. Now, *that* was what he called a view.

A moment later, she grabbed two plates from the buffet and handed one to him. "What should we try first? Any recommendations, since you've been here before?"

He pointed to a dish. "You should try that."

"Calamari?" Her nose wrinkled. "I've never been able to make myself go for squid. It sounds kind of nasty."

He scooped up a serving, set it on her plate and then did the same with his. "That's the beauty of a buffet. If you don't like it, you can still get other things."

"True." She cast the calamari a dubious glance, but then nodded firmly. "Okay. I'm on vacation. Let's go wild and try new things."

"I like the sound of that." His voice dropped to a low growl, and a dozen erotic possibilities paraded through his mind. His shaft began to harden and he forced himself to shut down that line of thought before he embarrassed himself in public.

A faint flush rose to her cheeks, and she licked her lips. "I didn't mean that in a sexual way."

"That's a shame." Winking at her, he strolled on to the next serving station. *Settle down, Lukas.* He swerved in and out of other diners to fill his plate and then wandered back to the table to find Julie was already there, sipping her lemonade.

When he sat down, she leaned back in her chair and studied him for a moment. He arched an eyebrow. "What? I haven't eaten anything yet, so there's no food on my face."

She tilted her head, and the smooth bell of her hair brushed against her shoulder. "No, but you have a slight accent and I can't figure out where you're from originally."

He stabbed a bite of ham from his plate. "Berlin, though I went to university in Heidelberg."

"That's where you became Dr. Klein?" She set down her drink and popped a cherry tomato from her salad into her mouth.

It took him a moment to answer because his gaze locked on the slow movement of her lips, the way her tongue darted out to catch a drop of dressing that had been on the tomato. The innocent gesture became sensual, and lust tightened his insides. He'd like her lips and tongue sliding over his skin in a far more intimate setting. He cleared his throat and returned his attention to her question. "*Nein,* that's where I got what you'd call a Master's degree in the U.S. My doctorate is from Harvard."

Her eyebrows winged upward. "Impressive."

"Thanks."

"Is that where you work now? Harvard?"

"Stanford, actually. So, like you, I'm not that far from San Francisco. Though the Bay Area covers quite a bit of territory." Which meant they might not live that close to each other, but they could also be next-door neighbors. The last prospect sounded far better than the first, and he knew it shouldn't. He'd been burned too badly in his last relationship to wish for another. Ever.

"I'm in Half Moon Bay, so it's—what—a half an hour drive to Palo Alto?" Something flashed in her gaze, and he had a feeling she was wondering if they might end up making that drive in the future. He refused to admit that he might have considered the possibility for a split second himself. Too soon to be thinking that way. Too soon and too dangerous for his peace of mind. A short tropical affair was all he'd be willing to pursue.

They both reached for the salt shaker at the same time and their fingers tangled. Neither of them pulled back, their gazes locking. Just that quickly, hot chemistry sizzled between them. He drew her hand slowly to his mouth, turned it over to brush his lips over her palm and bit down lightly on the base of her thumb. Raw want flashed across her expressive face. Answering need fisted in his gut, sent lava boiling through his veins. His body went rigid, his erection chafing against his fly. And that was when he knew without any doubts that this week was going to end with some serious mattress time. Bam. No more just hoping. He *knew*. The attraction was too powerful to resist.

"I want you." He said it bluntly but pitched his voice low enough so that no one could overhear. "I have since the minute I saw you. I'm telling you to make sure we're on the same page. If this is just a little harmless flirtation, that's fine, but I'd like more. The naked, sweaty kind of more. If you're not interested in that, let me know now."

She drew in a sharp breath that lifted her breasts against the front of her blouse. His gaze zeroed in on them, and he noticed that her nipples were hard points. He wanted to suck them. She tugged her hand from his grip and crossed her arms over her chest, rolling her eyes. "Clearly, I'm interested. Not...right this second, since we just met a few hours ago, but...I'd be lying if I said I wasn't thinking we'd end up in bed together."

God, yes. He'd love to see her tangled in his sheets, her dark hair spread out on a white pillowcase, her body arched to take him deep. Impossibly, inevitably, his erection grew harder, his lust skyrocketing. He craved this woman in a way he hadn't craved anyone in...years. Maybe ever. He had to have her. Sooner would be better than later.

She cleared her throat, glancing away. "So, um...I took a couple of semesters of German in college." Her hand made a graceful arc through the air as she spoke. "We had a foreign language requirement we had to fulfill, and I thought I might like to study abroad in Berlin someday."

"And how did you like my hometown?" He settled back in his seat, enjoying the way a blush stained her cheeks.

"I didn't end up going. My mother died and I decided leaving my dad behind for a year would be a bad idea." She shrugged, fidgeting in her seat. "I don't remember much German now though. Languages are a use-it or lose-it kind of skill, I suppose."

Sympathy and pain squeezed inside of him, and he reached over to curl his fingers over hers. "I'm sorry about your mom. I lost my dad a few years ago and...I'm sorry."

"Me too." She tightened her hand on his for a moment before she pulled back, and he thought he saw a glimmer of tears in her gaze before she blinked them away and offered up a brave grin. "Okay, let's lighten the moment a bit, shall we?"

The conversation had morphed from sexy to sad in moments, and he wasn't sure how to rein it back in to normalcy. The woman had a knack for keeping him off-balance. As someone who liked to be in control, that wasn't necessarily what he considered a good thing. "How should we do that?"

"Like this." She speared some of the calamari with her fork and lifted it for him to see. "The great experiment begins, Dr. Scientist. Ready?"

He arched a brow. "You realize for an experiment to be successful, you have to repeat it. Scientists have to be able to verify their findings."

She popped the food into her mouth. There was a long pause before horror crossed her expression. She looked as if she really wanted to spit it out, but then screwed up her face and began chewing rapidly. Choking a little when she swallowed, she dove for her drink. He couldn't help the laughter that spilled out of him, and he wrapped an arm around his stomach while another wave of chuckles broke loose.

"Blech. Nasty." She scrubbed her napkin over her mouth. "I'm not trying that again. The experiment was a *resounding* failure."

The look of offended dignity she turned on him just made him laugh harder, and he had to wipe tears from his eyes. "No squid for Julie. Got it."

She stuck her tongue out at him. "Don't take food recommendations from Lukas. Got it."

"Hey, I have excellent taste in food." He reached over the table and stabbed his fork into the remaining calamari on her plate. "I'm willing to eat everything I recommend."

He suited actions to words, snorting at the disgusted fascination on her face as she watched him chew and swallow. With a roll of her eyes, she went back to her own dinner. They settled into a companionable silence for a while, and it was far more comfortable than he would have anticipated. When they did talk, it was light. She regaled him with a few outrageous stories about her group of friends, and he made her chortle at some of his cultural misadventures when he'd first moved to the States. The conversation wasn't deep, but it was...nice. The meal was as delicious as he expected from the restaurant, despite the squid mishap, and he was with an intelligent, desirable woman. Not a bad way to spend the evening.

When the check arrived, they both reached for it, but he tugged it away from her. "I've got this."

She frowned. "We can split it. It's not like this is a date."

Raising an eyebrow, he tsked. "What makes you think it's not a date?"

"I..." She blinked. "Well, I guess it is, if we want it to be."

"I want." He offered her a look he knew was nothing short of wicked. "Didn't I already make that clear?"

The breath she let out was shaky. "Yes."

Whether she was agreeing to his clarity or to the wanting, he wasn't sure, but he knew which he was hoping for. Tossing a few bills on the table, he rose to his feet and held out his hand. "Come on, let's watch the last of the sunset on the beach."

Her slim fingers slipped into his, and he pulled her out of her seat. He kept his hold on her hand as they left the restaurant, and he liked the feel of her palm nestled against his. They stood on a wide concrete path that separated the hotel's property from the beach, and it seemed the world went quiet and still as everyone turned to watch the last sliver of the sun slip below the horizon.

"Gorgeous," Julie whispered beside him. "Just like on a postcard, it was so perfect."

"You've never been to Hawaii?" He glanced away from the fading rays of sunset to look at her.

She shook her head. "Nope."

"Then why come here for Christmas?" He frowned. "You might not even have liked it here. Not everyone cares for the crowds on Waikiki Beach."

"Because I *wanted* to go somewhere I'd never been before. I wasn't exactly feeling the spirit of the season." Shrugging, she met his gaze. "But the holidays are definitely starting to look up."

"You should like this, then." He pointed to a young Hawaiian man running down the beach with a torch in his hand. The man was in traditional island garb with a loincloth and fresh *ti* leaves wreathing his head, upper arms and ankles. Every few meters, he'd pause to light tiki torches that were buried in the sand. "They do this ritual at sunset. I've always thought it was an interesting tradition."

"Mmm-hmm. *Very* interesting." The lilt in Julie's voice made Lukas glance at her again.

"You like it?"

"Oh, yeah. But I think your enjoyment of it is a little different than mine. And every other heterosexual woman watching. The guy is ripped and half naked. Hello, Hawaiian fantasy man." A rich chuckle bubbled out of her, her dark gaze dancing with mirth, the firelight caressing the curves of her face. At that moment, she was the most intoxicating thing he'd ever seen.

CHAPTER THREE

H e had to kiss her. He couldn't help himself.

Brushing his lips over hers, he caught her laughter with his mouth. It was meant to be quick, fleeting. But he felt her breathing hitch, and her arms slid around his neck, bringing their bodies into full contact. He bit back a groan at having her softness molded to his harder planes. Rising up on tiptoe, she pressed closer, and nipped at his lower lip with her teeth. This time, he didn't bother to hold in the groan as he feasted on her mouth.

Thrusting his tongue between her lips, he savored the sweet flavor of her. He wrapped his arms around her, pulled her even tighter to him, and he skimmed his hands down her back. Touching her was the most erotic thing he'd done in years, and they weren't even naked yet. He curled his hands over her backside, rocking himself into the juncture of her thighs. More. God, he wanted inside her. He burned with the craving, his heart raced as hot blood pounded through his veins. She whimpered, her nails digging into his scalp as she pulled him nearer.

A little pain to sharpen the pleasure.

The sound of giggling brought his head up, reminding him of where they were and what they were doing. Fuck. He shot a glare at a couple of young teenagers who were staring at them. Suppressing a snarl, he slowly eased himself away from Julie. His body throbbed, and a shudder wracked him at the lust he had to deny.

"Wow. That was...wow." She drew in a shaky breath, her hands still clinging to his shoulders.

A snort escaped him and he shook his head. "I agree. We should do it again some time."

The teens giggled again, and Julie flushed, stepping back. Embarrassment flooded her expression, and he hated that. Her hands rose to smooth her hair and fuss with her clothes. "Um...I don't normally..."

"Make out on public beaches? Me neither. Exhibitionism isn't my style." Catching her arm, he guided her down a path away from their audience. "Would you care to have that drink now?"

"Okay." She glanced back as if she expected their nosy observers to have followed. "I know I'm the one who asked for the drink, but I have to admit I'm a lightweight when it comes to alcohol. One cocktail and I'm okay, two is iffy, and by the time I'm done with number three I'm dancing on the table with a lampshade on my head."

"Now there's a show I'd like to see." And he'd enjoy every minute of it too. He tugged her forward, leading her past a pond with flamingos. "But you can have a soda, if you prefer. There's an interesting Hawaiian band playing tonight in the Tapa Bar. Olomana, they're called. I like their music."

"Sounds great." She glanced around. They approached a space with a stage set up on one side, a bar on the other, and tables in between. One of the hotel towers soared overhead and provided a roof, but other than pillars to hold up the building, the bar had no walls. "This place is pretty cool."

"I've always liked it." The band was already playing and it was standing room only, but he spotted a couple leaving their table and urged Julie in that direction. Perfect timing. He pulled out a chair for her, motioning her into it.

"Thanks." She settled into the seat, her gaze going to the stage. They sat in silence for a moment while the song wound down. She turned her head to look at him. "Do you come to Hawaii often, Lukas?"

He rocked a hand back and forth through the air. "My conference is here every year. I don't always attend, but when I do, I try to find time to relax. This is one of the places I do that."

"Well, this is my first time, and I want to make the most of it." She narrowed her gaze at him. "Don't you dare make a virgin joke out of that."

His grin was wolfish. "I wouldn't dream of it."

"Liar," she retorted softly, her eyes crinkling in amusement.

"Aloha. Welcome to the Tapa Bar." A waitress bustled up, picking up the glasses from the table's last occupants and wiping down the wooden surface. "So, what can I get you two?"

Julie leaned forward, and he got a clear shot at her cleavage. Damn, he wanted his hands on those breasts. He wanted to know what color her nipples were, if they'd turn red for him when he sucked them.

She waved a hand. "I want something that's an island classic. What would you recommend?"

"A Blue Hawaiian, Pineapple Margarita, or Lava Flow." The waitress tilted her head. "Maybe a Mai Tai."

Julie pursed her lips. "I've had a Mai Tai and a margarita before, but I'm debating between the Lava Flow and the Blue Hawaiian."

"We'll take one of each, and we can share." He pushed his fingers through his hair, trying to rein in the desire to forget the drinks and drag her back to his room. It had been a while since he'd indulged in an affair, but his body was more than eager to give it a try. With Julie. "How does that sound?"

"I'm game." She smiled at him, and it was a kick to the chest. She was so lovely and he wanted her.

The waitress left, but he barely spared her a glance. His attention was on the woman before him. "You said you came here because you weren't in the holiday spirit. What happened?"

Her chin lifted. "How do you know something happened?"

"Because you seem the type of woman who enjoys life, celebrates it." A few minutes with her had told him that. A woman who laughed at the rain and sighed over a beautiful sunset wasn't bored by the world around her. "I'm guessing you don't just *like* the holidays, you're the first one on your street with lights and a tree up every year. Am I right?"

She made a face at him. "Maybe."

"So, something had to have happened. There's a story there." He crooked a finger at her. "Tell me."

Why he was so insistent, he wasn't sure. He liked to solve puzzles, liked everything to make sense, but he didn't normally push for people to spill their problems all over him. Out of character, but he couldn't deny he wanted to know more about her, what made her tick.

"Yeah, okay, so I like holidays. I get that from my great-aunt, Eloise, I guess. She was *huge* on Christmas." She dropped a shoulder in a shrug, sadness filling her gaze. "She passed away in February. It was...difficult to lose her. She played a big part in my life."

Her mother and then her aunt? That was hard. His chest cinched tight. The unfamiliar need to comfort swamped him. He wanted to pull her into his arms and tell her it would all be okay, but that wasn't true. "I'm sorry for your many losses."

"Thank you." She tried for a smile, but didn't quite make it. "What about you? No family for the holidays?"

"My mother still lives in Berlin, but she's gotten too old to fly overseas any more, and the timing of my conference made it difficult to make it home." His mother had many, many friends she spent her holidays with. A brigade of retired women. Likely he'd have a difficult time even getting to speak to her on the phone to wish her a Merry Christmas. She had a more active social life than he did. "There are a few distant cousins in Frankfurt, but I haven't seen them since I was a small child."

"You said you were single, so that means no wife or girlfriend, but...no kids to spend Christmas with either?" Julie's eyebrows lifted.

He shrugged, the motion rougher than he would have liked. "I had a wife, but we divorced...five years ago, now. I like children, but I'm glad we didn't have any together."

"Ugly breakup?"

"Very." He didn't say more. He'd never told anyone exactly how bad the breakup had been, how gutted he'd been in the end. He only knew he couldn't live through something like that again.

Her dark gaze warmed. "I'm sorry you had to go through that."

He glanced away, dragging in a breath. "Me too."

She scooted her chair around the table so she sat next to him, her arm pressed to his. She said nothing else, but he could feel the empathy radiating from her. It was comforting. She was better at that than he was.

Leaning closer, she let her head rest on his shoulder. The softness of her pressed against him made his ugly memories dissipate, and his attention focused on here and now. Her nearness and the female scent of her made his body react in predictable ways.

Why he responded so strongly to her, he didn't know. He looked down at her, studying her when she seemed unaware of it. She wasn't the most beautiful woman he'd ever seen, but she got to him. It wasn't logical or rational. It wasn't like him. That realization gave him pause. Perhaps this was more dangerous than he wanted to consider. He watched her relax and enjoy the music, only barely noticing when the waitress returned with their drinks. Julie sipped hers, but Lukas just observed her as if that might make his scientist brain work out the puzzle. He'd already wondered if he might see her after they went back to California, but he had to dismiss that. It smacked of more commitment than he could offer any woman. His ex-wife had ensured that. He'd walked away from relationships and never looked back.

But Julie...he'd met her only a few hours before and she'd already taken hold of something inside him. The logical, rational thing to do would be to run if he wanted to be certain that nothing shook his conviction to keep away from commitment. The possibility that she could tempt him was real, that much he knew.

"The band is awesome. Thank you for suggesting this place." Reaching over, she twined her fingers with his, and it felt like the most natural thing in the world.

Dangerous, his mind whispered. But too good to pass up. Shouldn't he at least try the experience? If he discounted that they lived near each other, there was already a time limit. They were both in Hawaii for the holidays, and that was all he'd allow himself to consider. He'd do best to enjoy the time while it lasted...and he had no doubt he would enjoy Julie, in bed and out of it, but just for this handful of days.

Anything else was far too serious for him.

The alcohol warmed Julie's insides. Just enough to relax her muscles and let the music slide over her, every care drifting away. The band played holiday tunes with a Hawaiian flavor, and sang original songs in the Hawaiian language. It was lively and fun and made her tap her feet to the beat. Lukas looked just a little too somber, so she smiled at him, squeezing his hand. He grinned back, and that was nice. It was even nicer when he lifted her fingers to his lips and brushed a kiss over her knuckles.

"Are you having a good time?" She gestured to the bright blue cocktail in front of him. "You haven't touched your drink."

"The first sip is for you, so you can try both." He pushed the glass toward her. "We're sharing, remember?"

"I warned you what happens when I drink too much." She picked up the cocktail and took a swig anyway. Sweet and cold, with a kick of pineapple and coconut flavor. She had no idea what made it blue, but it was a tasty drink. She passed the Lava Flow to Lukas. "Your turn."

The corners of his eyes crinkled and he reached for the red cocktail. "I'm normally a beer drinker. Pilsner, hefeweizen...the good stuff. It's part of German genetics."

"You don't like American beer?" The tiny note of superiority in his voice made her bite back a giggle as he took a sip of the very girly mixed drink.

"Not the big U.S. brands." He gestured with the glass, still looking aggrieved. "It's all yellow water. That's not real beer."

She was proud of herself for keeping a straight face. "I'm glad there are imported options for you, then."

"You're mocking me." He gave her a stony stare.

"Maybe a little."

He stole the Blue Hawaiian from her, so he had both cocktails. "I think you've had enough. Clearly, your thinking is fuzzy or you'd understand how important good beer is to a well functioning society."

That was it, she couldn't hold back anymore. She laughed in his face, but held up her hands in surrender. "Okay, okay. I understand not to tease you about your beer anymore. Hand over the Lava Flow."

"I'm not sure that's good enough." His blue eyes narrowed, his expression calculating. "It'll cost you a kiss."

Heart thumping hard, she struggled to catch her breath, the low simmer of heat that hadn't quit since he'd kissed her—hell, since they'd met—firing high and hot within her. She licked her lips, and his gaze zeroed in on the movement, making it a far more sensual gesture than she'd meant it to be. Desire suffused her, loosening some muscles, tightening others.

"Just one kiss?"

His gaze rose from her lips to meet her eyes. "One will do. For now."

As she shifted in her seat to face him, her arm slid against his and her breast pressed to his side. His breathing hitched and his pupils expanded until only a thin ring of blue remained, lust flushing the sharp angles of his face. A delicious shiver went through her. Leaning in, she brushed her mouth over his. The brief contact made her lips tingle. She nibbled at his lower lip, letting the flavor of him seep into her senses. Sweet alcohol and something that was pure Lukas. Hot, masculine. Intoxicating.

Nipping soft kisses over his lips, down to his chin, and along his jaw, she felt his chest expand in a deep breath, heard him swallow hard when she bit his earlobe. He set the drinks on the table and grabbed the ledge with a white-knuckled grip. Heady power rushed through her, that she could make him react to her. Only the knowledge that they were in public stopped her from doing things that might get him to beg for more.

He dropped one hand to her bare knee to squeeze lightly before his fingers began to stroke her skin along the edge of her skirt. She closed her eyes as he drew circles on her flesh, her heart picking up speed to race in her chest. Anticipation stretched her nerves taut. Would he slide his hand up her skirt? She shivered at the thought, her nipples beading into hard peaks. White-hot flames licked at her insides, melting her core. Everything within her was focused on where he'd touch her next. She squeezed her legs together, savoring the ache between them. She froze as his fingers drifted ever higher, nudging the hem of her skirt up, and air brushed against her thighs.

It shocked her that she was letting a man she'd just met stroke her this way. Intimately. And she wanted more. No one had ever gotten to her this fast. Sure, she'd figured they might end up in bed before the end of the trip, but before the night was over? Definitely hadn't crossed her mind. Until now. He scraped her lightly with his nails, and moisture flooded her sex at the rougher contact.

Oh. God.

It was too much. Far, far too much. And nowhere near enough. Desperate need careened through her, a craving that couldn't be ignored. She wanted more. Now. She couldn't wait.

She clamped her hand over his wrist to still his movements, suppressing a shudder. "Let's go back to my room."

"No, mine," he whispered. "I have condoms. Do you?"

"No, I don't." She leaned back a little so she could look at his face. "You were expecting to get laid on vacation?"

"No." He took her hand and bit the base of her thumb, sending a pulse of heat exploding through her. "But I keep a couple in my travel kit, just in case."

"Well, thank God for being prepared." She grabbed her bag and stood. "Let's go."

Was this the wisest thing she'd ever done? Probably not. Was she going to do it anyway? Hell yes. Her hormones did a tap dance in joyful agreement.

She'd promised herself when she came here that she'd make an effort to get back to the land of the living. Loss and grief had taken the last year from her, and Auntie Eloise would have hated that. The old lady had always been one to relish every second. Julie could learn a thing or two from her example. So she was cutting loose and living in the moment.

She doubted she'd have any regrets in the morning either.

"This way." His hand splayed over the small of her back as he guided her through the sprawling hotel complex. His touch sent goose bumps rippling across her skin.

Every step made her thighs brush together, intensifying her cravings. The warm night breeze caressed her legs and arms, and she drew in a breath of soft sea air. It smelled different from home, but she liked it.

They passed a few people on the way to the Rainbow Tower, but when they reached the elevator bank, there was no one around. He pushed the button to call the car, then pressed her against the wall. The full-body contact made her moan, stoking the fire that already threatened to consume her. She stroked her hands down the planes of his back, loving the play of muscles under his shirt. He buried his face in her throat, his teeth sinking into the sensitive tendon that connected neck to shoulder. Heat dampened her core at the sweet pain shivering through her.

"Lukas, please," she whispered.

"Pleasing you is on the agenda, yes." His tongue trailed upward until he sucked her earlobe into his mouth.

"Oooh." She bunched her fingers in his shirt, arching against his body. She honestly didn't know how long she'd last before she dragged him into the bushes and had her way with him.

The elevator arrived, sending agony and relief whipping through her. Agony that they had to stop, relief that they could get to his room and those condoms *now*.

It took only thirty seconds to ride up the many floors to his room. While he was unlocking his door, she let her palm slide down his back to ass, boldly squeezing the curve of muscle there. He hissed in a breath, shuddering. Touching him was a turn-on, his reaction an even bigger one. After shoving open the door, he snaked an arm around her waist and dragged her over the threshold.

"This is crazy." She said it because she had to put it out there.

"It is." His embrace tightened until her breasts flattened to his chest. "But I don't want to stop."

"Me neither." No, this was a wild roller coaster she wanted to ride to the end. Her body was in wholehearted agreement, every point of contact between them sending ripples of heated awareness shooting through her.

"Good," he growled. The door swung closed, a light flipped on, and she was alone with him. Excitement spurted inside her, sharpening the edge of her need. Her breathing sped, her skin feeling as if it were aflame. He brushed his lips over hers in a fleeting gesture before he released her. "Condoms—we'll need them. Give me one minute."

He walked into the bathroom, and she did a slow spin to take in his room. It looked much like hers, though his windows faced a different direction. She thought his might overlook the ocean, where hers had a view of Diamond Head, but it was too dark out now for her to be sure. A discarded shirt lay over his chair and a laptop sat on the desk, but the rest of his belongings were out of sight. She snorted softly.

"What?" A brawny arm wrapped around her waist as he came up behind her and kissed the back of her neck.

"I think we have the same laptop." She waved a hand toward the small desk.

"Do we?" She felt him grin against her skin. Then he bit her nape and all thoughts of computers dissipated. "Great minds think alike."

She shivered when his teeth scraped her flesh. His palm pressed to her belly, edged under her top, burning against the skin of her midriff, and she bit her lower lip as he moved higher. The air tangled in her throat and she shut her eyes to let herself savor the rush of feelings, so sweet and hot. His hand curved around her breast, cupping her through the lace of her bra just long enough to make her quiver with anticipation, aching to have him touch her flesh. After dipping into her bra, his fingers closed over her nipple, pinching, twisting, and a gasp strangled out of her. Letting her head fall back on his shoulder, she grabbed his thighs. "Lukas."

"Mmm?" His tongue slid up the side of her throat, and he nipped at her ear. Her sex clenched in helpless reaction, and she could feel how slick she was—needy and greedy.

Her hands gripped his legs tighter, anchoring herself to sanity. "I want..."

"You want?" His voice rasped her ear, his breathing as ragged as hers. "Tell me, Julie."

His accent had thickened with his passion, rolling her name into something exotic. He pinched her nipple hard and she cried out. "More! I want more. Please, Lukas."

"Yes." The word was gritted out, and he spun her around to back her toward the bed. The lamplight cast harsh shadows on his face, making the angles of his jaw and cheekbones sharper. He looked predatory, possessive, and it made her heart pound.

He dropped a handful of condoms on the nightstand, then pulled his shirt over his head and tossed it aside. She let her gaze roam over his bare chest, which was muscular and sprinkled with just the right amount of hair. Humming in approval, she reached out to test the width of his shoulders, tracing the hardness of his collarbone. He tugged at the bottom of her shirt, drawing it upward until she had to stop touching him long enough to let him get the garment over her head. Her hands went back to their exploration, and she spread her fingers over his pecs, the crisp curls tickling her palms.

The pad of her thumb rubbed over his nipple and the flat disc beaded for her, a shudder rippling through him. His hands clutched at her hips, his fingers digging in until it was almost painful. Almost. Under her palms, she felt the way his heart raced. His reaction sent a pulse of need through her, fueling her blood. He fumbled for the zipper on the back of her skirt, and she wriggled to let the circle of fabric pool at her feet. His hands closed over her ass, kneading the twin globes. She clenched her teeth on a whimper when he eased under the elastic band of her underwear, dipping into her sex from behind. Oh. *God*.

"So wet." His breath hissed in, and he stroked her damp lips, circling her core. More moisture gushed from her, and the muscles in her thighs shook. How much longer she could stay upright, she wasn't sure. Her body burned as he teased her sex. But two could play this game. She bent forward, flicking her tongue against the tight little bud of his nipple, sucking on him.

A groan rumbled in his chest, vibrating against her lips. Then she bit down. Hard.

He jerked, swore. Two fingers boldly penetrated her sex, and her legs gave out from under her. "Lukas!"

"Yes. Now." He stripped her panties off and shoved her back so that she bounced against the mattress. She watched as he unbuckled his belt, unfastened his pants, and kicked out of his shoes. He was naked in seconds, and her gaze caught on the impressive arc of his erection. Long, thick and perfect.

"I won't last longer than a minute if you keep looking at me like that, *mein Liebling*."

She licked her lips, letting her thighs fall open in blatant invitation. "What's that mean?"

"You're killing me." A harsh sound came from his throat. "It basically means my darling or sweetheart."

One long arm reached out and snagged a condom off the nightstand. He rolled it on and knelt on the bed between her legs, his gaze searing into her flesh as he took her body in. After tugging the straps of her bra down, he peeled the cups away from her breasts. "So beautiful."

Bending over her, he sucked one peak into his mouth, his tongue batting at her nipple. Sensation shot straight from breast to loin, and her sex fisted on emptiness. God, she needed to be filled. She was wet, ready. Arching beneath him, she tried to pull him down to her. She wanted him on her, in her. *Now.*

He shoved her nipple against the roof of his mouth, and a high, thin scream broke from her throat. Her nails scored into his back. "Please, please, *please.*"

Releasing her breast, he moved to settle himself fully atop her. Finally. His lips possessed her, his tongue thrusting into her mouth. The blunt probing of his shaft against her slick folds made her moan against his lips. She wrapped her legs around his waist, tilting her hips up in offering. He pushed the first inch into her, withdrew, entered her again, deeper this time. Her inner muscles squeezed around the thickness of his shaft, trying to draw him in. The stretch was exquisite, made her whimper when he was seated fully within her.

So full, so perfect. But it wasn't enough. She needed to come—her body craved it, demanded it. Undulating beneath him, she tried to convey what she needed. She opened her mouth on his shoulder, biting down on the saltiness of his flesh.

"Hurry *up*, Lukas."

"Jesus," he groaned, but he gave her what she wanted. She pressed her palms against his back, feeling the play of muscles under his skin as his thrusts picked up speed and force. The slap of their skin, the squeak of the mattress beneath them, the harsh gasping of their breath as they moved echoed in the room. A symphony of carnal pleasure. It was beyond erotic—the sound, the scent. Sex and Lukas.

Sweat slid in rivulets down her skin, making their bodies glide together. The hair on his chest stimulated her nipples and added another layer to the sensations bombarding her. She arched into him to meet each downward plunge of his hips, her sex contracting when he filled her. Orgasm built, shivers running along her limbs. She wanted to go over that edge with him. Her cravings sharpened to a white-hot blade that sliced through her. She was so very close. She curled her nails into his back and raked them down his skin.

He froze, and the sound he made was like a human volcano erupting. Then he pounded into her, his movements rough and as desperate as she felt. It was almost painful, but just merged with her desire, heightened the intensity. He angled his pelvis, grinding down on her sex.

It was enough. More than enough.

She exploded, her channel fisting around his shaft in rhythmic waves. A moan spilled from her throat, her hips snapped up to meet his continued thrusts, and he dragged out her climax as long as possible. Each time he entered her, aftershocks of orgasm shook her. The clench and release of her inner muscles went on forever, left her giddy with ecstasy.

A massive shudder wracked his big body and he jutted his length deeper inside her. He moaned, the sound escaping between clenched teeth. Those sharp blue eyes of his lost focus, and she watched him come, loving that she could reduce the rational professor to nothing but animalistic need. It was an incredible rush. He hung above her for a long moment before he sank down on top of her, his face buried in the crook of her neck. The air conditioner kicked on and she shivered, flattening her palms to his shoulders. The contrast of heated skin and cool air made her skin prickle. She sighed and closed her eyes, letting bliss unfurl inside of her. Damn, she felt *good*.

Time stretched, became elastic. She had no idea how many minutes passed before he leveraged himself away from her, rolling to his side to lie next to her. Propped up on his forearm, he stared down at her. His eyes were half-lidded and one corner of his mouth kicked up.

"That was...amazing." A huge yawn cracked his jaw, and he chuckled. "It's a miracle I'm still awake." He rolled to his feet with easy masculine grace and moved toward the bathroom. "I need to clean up. I'll be back in a moment."

When the door closed behind him and she had a moment to herself, a tiny niggle of doubt assailed her. Did he want her to stay the night or was mentioning how tired he was a subtle cue for her to leave? She hadn't done a one-night stand since her junior year of college, so she was more than a little rusty on the protocol. Should she get her stuff and go? The thought depressed her. But she sat up, pushed her hair out of her face, and looked over the side of the bed for her clothes.

The sound of water running and the toilet flushing reached her, then Lukas flipped the bathroom door open. He yawned again, scrubbing a hand down his face. His grin was rueful. "Promise you won't be offended if I pass out on you right away?"

She swallowed, glancing aside. "Would you prefer I left so you can sleep alone?"

"No." He nudged her over on the mattress and sprawled beside her. "If I wanted that, I would have said so. What I want is—"

"For me not to be offended when you pass out on me." The relief that hit her was a little too overwhelming. He wanted her to stay, and that mattered far more than it should. She suppressed that alarming thought.

"Yes." He kissed her shoulder, wrapped an arm around her, and tucked her in close to his chest. His voice slowed with incipient slumber. "Also, I'd like you to go swimming with me."

Her eyebrows drew together, confusion spinning within her. She twisted her torso to get a look at his face. Was he talking in his sleep now? "Huh?"

But his eyes were still open and focused on her. "I swim in the ocean in the mornings. It's warm, even in winter. Come with me tomorrow."

She blinked. "I'd like that."

"Good." His arm tightened around her as if he had no intention of letting her leave. "*Gute Nacht, mein Liebling*."

"*Gute Nacht*." A sigh eased out of her, and she shook her head. Her body ached pleasantly, the way it should after a bout of explosive sex. It had been amazing, just as he'd said. She'd loved it. Every second of it. The powerful emotional reaction was just her hormones going into overdrive. She hadn't been intimate with anyone since before Eloise died, so of course this would hit her harder than normal. Closing her eyes, she let herself enjoy the feel of his arms around her. This was nice, but it was temporary. Vacation fling—that was all she wanted. Loosen up, live a little. Then go home and get back to her life, her friends, her shop.

As if her thought had somehow reached Half Moon Bay, her phone jingled with the text message alert she had for her friends. She tensed, waiting to see if the sound had woken Lukas. He didn't so much as twitch. Slipping out of his embrace meant she could go in search of her cell. She flipped it to silent mode before it could chime a reminder.

Meg's number showed on her display. *Hey, sweetie. I'm hanging out with the girls. Slumber party! How was your first day in paradise? Do anything fun? Deets needed!*

Before Julie could respond, her phone vibrated, and Anne's name popped up. *Forget Meg! Tell me if you found the hot cabana boy yet.*

Biting her lip to keep from laughing, Julie glanced over at the sleeping Lukas. She hesitated for a moment before she responded, not quite ready to tell her friends about him. They'd want details she couldn't bring herself to share. Maybe tomorrow. After she'd gotten used to the idea of her island affair. She grinned. It sounded lush and exotic, not like her at all.

Pushing a few buttons on her phone, she sent out a joint reply to Meg, Anne, and Karen. *First day was awesome! I'm going swimming in the ocean in the morning. It's bikini weather here. You know you're jealous! No cabana boy so far, but there was a half-naked hottie lighting tiki torches.*

There. Not a lie, but not the whole truth. Not yet. She shut her phone down, set it on the nightstand and crawled back into bed.

Lukas pulled her close again, his sleepy voice low in her ear. "Everything all right?"

"Yeah," she replied. "Everything is fine. My friends were just checking in."

She had good friends, a fantastic new lover, and a week left to enjoy him, since he seemed to want to spend more time with her. Everything was more than *fine*. Life was pretty damn awesome right now. It'd been a while since she could say that, so she let herself embrace the moment.

Without a doubt, this was going to be a vacation to remember. If this was just day one, she couldn't wait to see what tomorrow had in store for her.

CHAPTER FOUR

"**H**ey."

Someone's fingertip gently traced the curve of Lukas's eyebrow. He opened his eyes and found Julie kneeling on the bed beside him. She was dressed, and that made him frown in confusion. "Hi..."

The corners of her mouth quirked. "I know it's barely dawn, but I'm still on California time and I can't sleep another wink." That fingertip stroked between his brows and down the bridge of his nose. "You were exhausted and I want you to keep sleeping, but I need to get up. I'm heading back to my room, taking a shower, then going to the pool with a good book for some sunbathing. When you're fully awake, give me a call and we'll do that ocean swim."

He swallowed, licked his lips, and tried to focus his blurry mind. It was a futile effort—his body had decided sleep was the priority and it was already trying to drag him back into unconsciousness. "Okay. Sorry I'm so tired."

"No worries." She bent down to brush her lips over his. "I wrote my number on the notepad on the desk. Call me."

"I will."

He was already asleep before she left the room.

When he managed to pry his eyes open again, the sun was shooting shafts of light between the curtains. He sighed, stretched and grinned. Damn, he felt good. He hadn't slept that well in months. It was hard to contemplate dragging his carcass out of bed when he was so comfortable. He lay there for a few more minutes, letting the last twenty-four hours run through his mind. Frenetic, but good. It had definitely ended on a high point.

His stomach rumbled and his body jangled for caffeine. Time to get up. And when he was up, there was Julie. Waiting for him. He liked that thought. Even more, he liked that she hadn't seemed upset when he'd been more interested in sleep than her. He winced, but it was the truth. Sometimes the body needed what it needed. A week with little slumber followed by energetic sex meant he'd crashed hard.

He'd been with women who would have been seriously pissed that he'd passed out on them. Twice, if he counted the post-sex pass out the night before. He hoped Julie had been sincere when she'd said not to worry about it. He liked her—maybe a little more than he should—and didn't relish the idea of awkwardness between them. Then again, he didn't enjoy hurting women's feelings in general. One more reason to avoid serious entanglements with them—the longer he was around them, the more likely it was that things would blow up in his face.

He scrubbed a hand over his hair, pushing those thoughts away. There was only one certain way to find out if Julie was as nonchalant as she seemed. He threw back the covers and rolled to his feet. Caffeine was the first order of business. He set the coffeemaker in the room on to perk, brushed his teeth, and then went to the desk to find Julie's number. After picking up his cell phone, he sent her a text.

I'm coherent now. Where would you like to meet for that swim?

Her response came back within ten seconds. *I'm lounging by the main pool.*

Give me fifteen minutes and I'll be there. After he sent the final text, he set his phone aside and went into the bathroom.

Anticipation warmed his chest. The thought of Julie's curves showcased by the thin material of a bathing suit was enough to have his body stirring with interest. He grabbed his swim trunks from where he'd left them hanging to dry over the shower rod the morning before. It took a few minutes to suck down the hot coffee, and then he was out the door in search of Julie.

When he found her, she was lying face down on a lounger with a towel draped around her. She had a Kindle in her hands and was so engrossed in what she was reading she didn't notice his approach. Her knees bent and her feet lifted in the air, her toes curling and she grinned at something in her book. The bare length of her legs caught his attention and he vividly remembered them wrapped around his waist the night before. The memory was enough to have him salivating, and he had to swallow before he could speak.

"What are you reading?" There, that was a safe enough question, with nothing sexual to it. He'd rather not embarrass himself by walking around with an enormous erection. His shorts wouldn't hide anything.

She jerked a bit, obviously startled, but then turned her head and grinned at him. "A filthy romance novel. It's awesome."

So much for a non-sexual question. Now he was wondering how many fantasies such a novel could give her, and how many of them he could help her fulfill in the next week.

Down boy.

She licked her lower lip. "I bought it just before I left because it got a great review on *Smart Bitches, Trashy Books*."

"*Smart*...uh, never mind. Don't tell me." He held up his hands, dropping onto the empty lounger next to her. "I'm glad you're enjoying your book."

Her eyebrows arched. "Well, what do *you* read for fun?"

"For this trip, I brought along a Wallander mystery from Henning Mankell. In German." Definitely not the kind of book to fuel sexual fantasies, but it was his favorite genre. A nice release from the more technical reading for his research.

She pursed her lips. "Mystery, huh?"

"Yes." He shrugged. "It's an amazing series with themes that really speak to some of the problems in Europe. Immigration from former colonies, and a resulting increase in crime, but also intolerance and racism."

"Sounds pretty dark."

"But realistic. I like that about the books."

She waved her Kindle in the air. "I like my books with happy endings. It's a nice break from reality, which I can get a nasty dose of by turning on the news."

Nodding, he conceded the point. "I can see the appeal in that. I like my mysteries, even if they are less rosy."

"The bad guys still get caught," she pointed out. "So that's still kind of a happy ending."

"*Happy* is a bit of a stretch." He propped his foot on his lounger and draped his forearm over his bent knee. "But I enjoy it anyway."

"Where is the series set in Germany?" She tilted a shoulder forward, and the towel covering slipped down to reveal a bit of her smooth back. "I imagine it gives you a nice dose of home."

"It's set in Sweden, actually. I just read the German translations."

"Oh, like those *Girl with the Dragon Tattoo* books. They're Swedish too." She turned on her side to face him, and he regretted that the towel moved with her and he didn't get to see what kind of bathing suit she was wearing.

He forced his focus to her face. Books. They were having a very pleasant discussion about books, not the fact that he liked to have sex in the morning. Or what her favorite position was. Or whether her room was closer than his and how quickly they could get to one of them. He cleared his throat. "Yes, I read that series. Sweden has produced some great crime novelists. Denmark too, actually."

Making a mock-concerned face, she said, "Scandinavians suddenly sound like a creepier and more sinister bunch than I thought."

He laughed. "Not really. Most Scandinavian countries I've visited are very safe."

Her brow scrunched. "So they make up crime fiction since they don't have any in real life?"

"Something like that." He let his foot drop to the floor. "So, what do you have planned for your week here? Other than a sea swim with me."

He shouldn't ask. That kind of question invited someone to think he might be interested joining in on those plans, which he shouldn't be. But he was. He didn't bother lying to himself about it. He blew out a breath. Okay, so this island affair might be a little more involved than the occasional dinner and mindless sex whenever they weren't otherwise occupied. Not what he'd thought at first, but he could adjust. He didn't want this interlude to end. Being around her was too sweet to give it up just yet.

Her mouth formed a thoughtful moue. "Well, I wanted to take it easy the first twenty-four hours. I don't have anything solid on the agenda until tomorrow."

"What's tomorrow?"

She propped her head in her palm. "Pearl Harbor."

"Ah, the classic." If it was her first trip, it was an obvious choice. He'd made that pilgrimage his first time too.

"Exactly." She wagged a finger at him.

He thought twice before he opened his mouth, but then he said, "If it sounds appealing, you could join me today. I was thinking about catching a bus to go downtown. The Iolani Palace is there and I've never been."

"Oooh, so you'd be a virginal tourist like me, huh?" She waggled her eyebrows.

He chuckled. "Care to lose your virginity with me?"

She widened her eyes. "It has to be better than the ping pong table in my neighbor's basement where I really lost my virginity."

A loud guffaw broke from him and he shook his head. "Any response I can think of to that is just highly inappropriate. Want to go for that swim now?"

"I would, actually." She winked. Tossing the towel aside, she stood.

When he got a good look at what she was wearing, his jaw sagged. He gave her a more thorough and appreciative examination. Her hair was pulled into two short ponytails behind each ear, which made her look like a teenager. But that wasn't what caught his attention. He waved a hand at her swimsuit. "What is this?"

"A crochet bikini." She ran a finger along the tie at one hip. "I designed the pattern for it over a year ago, but didn't have a reason to wear it until now."

Slender crisscrossing strands formed tantalizing patterns that shaped around her breasts on top and over her ass and between her legs on the bottom. The whole thing was held together by braded cords that fastened at each hip and behind her neck. The cut wasn't immodest, but it fit her every curve to perfection, and there was something about the material—as if it was so delicate it might tear away at any moment. He couldn't take his eyes off it, hoping for that fateful moment.

He licked his lips. "You *made* this?"

"Well, yeah." She shrugged. "What did you think a fiber artist did?"

"I had no idea." He reached out to slide his thumb along the same tie, dropping his voice to a low timbre. "But I'm in favor of any profession that creates something this sinful."

She flushed. "Thank you. I think."

"So tell me what a fiber artist does." He slipped an arm around her waist and guided her toward the water's edge.

"Well, first and foremost, I run a fiber arts store." She tucked a lock of escaped hair behind her ear. "Actually, since Aunt Eloise died, I guess I own *and* run a fiber arts store. It's a business, like any other."

"A successful business, I'm guessing." Especially if she sold confections like the one she was wearing. Every woman on the planet should have one.

She shrugged modestly. "Purl Moon has done pretty well, even in the crappy economy. I took the business online in the last year, so we get orders from all over the world now. That's helped boost our profit margin."

"You still haven't answered my question. What exactly does a fiber artist do?" He kissed the side of her neck, just above the tie, and a shiver coursed through her.

"Okay, the simplest explanation is: I get raw fibers from different kinds of sheep, goats, and even rabbits." She lifted a finger. "Oh, and some plants too, like bamboo. I dye them by hand and spin them into yarn that I can sell or use to knit, crochet, felt or tat into products I can wear, give as gifts, display as samples, or sell to customers. That's generally what a fiber artist does." She tipped her head, eyebrows scrunching. "But I also buy and sell a lot of yarns that I don't make myself. And I teach classes on how to do all of those things—spin, knit, crochet, etcetera."

He blinked. "Impressive."

"Thanks." She dimpled. "This bikini is made of cotton, so it doesn't get as waterlogged or stretchy as other fibers, which means you can actually swim in it, rather than just sunbathe." She gave him a look. "Or pose for a gentleman's viewing pleasure."

"It is a pleasure, indeed. You're right about that." If he didn't stop staring at her soon, his erection would be straining the confines of his trunks in very visible ways. "Let's test the swimability of your creation."

Maybe by the time they got out of the water, he'd have calmed down a bit. It was a pretty futile hope with this woman nearby, but he didn't have much choice. The water closed around him, feeling far too cold against his heated skin. It would only take a few minutes to adjust, fortunately, because he shuddered at the first submersion.

It wasn't until he was waist-deep that he realized any fear he'd had about her being uptight over the passing-out-on-her incidents had dissipated. Being around her was...easy. Fun. He couldn't remember the last time he could say that about any woman he had a romantic interest in. His past experiences had left him jaded and wary, but Julie was *nice*, for lack of a better word. She made him laugh. He didn't know what that would mean, in the end, but if things kept going the way they were, it was going to be an unforgettable holiday.

"Brr." Julie shivered as she waded into the water next to Lukas, crossing her arms over her chest. Which covered her puckered nipples, thank God. The moment he'd looked at her bikini, fire had licked through her veins. She was honest enough to know she'd chosen to wear this suit because she'd hoped he'd have exactly that kind of reaction. A woman liked to be appreciated, but she'd underestimated her body's response to the lust that had molded his sensuous features. The shock of ocean water was probably the best thing for her, or she might have jumped him right there on the lounger. The hotel probably looked unfavorably on that kind of public indecency. She rubbed her hands up and down her biceps, battling the goose bumps. "Okay, definitely warmer than California waters, but still chilly."

"Moving helps." He kicked off, heading toward a pier made of piled volcanic rocks. He glanced back with a little grin. "Coming?"

The low growl to the word made it sound far more like a sexual invitation than it should have, but that might just be her own lascivious thoughts giving it the prurient twist. "Right behind you."

The waves lapped around her shoulders and face, but the exercise dispelled the cold. Julie kept pace with him until they drew up at a reef that curved past the end of the pier. It seemed to be more volcanic rock than reef, but there were definitely plants growing in it and she could see a few small fish whipping through the clear water below her. She wished she had a snorkel and mask so she could see more.

She pressed her hands to the top of the reef, steadying herself as a wave washed over it.

"At low tide, the reef is barely covered by water and people can walk on top of it. They usually just hop down from there." Lukas gestured to the pier. "I've never tried it since it looks rough on the feet, but the kids who come out seem to love it."

"The water is so clear, even this far away from shore. It's almost gray in Half Moon Bay." Julie swept her arm through the waves to demonstrate her point.

"And much nicer to swim in than the Baltic, which is where we vacationed when I was a child."

The next wave came in a little rougher than the last, and pushed her toward the shore. He caught her around the waist and towed her into his embrace. A little hum of pleasure escaped her and she hooked an arm behind his neck, pressing her front to his chest. This was where she'd wanted to be since the moment she'd woken beside him this morning. Back in his arms. He glanced down, and she was betting he got an eyeful of her cleavage. The heat in his gaze made it clear he liked what he saw.

A quick glance told her there was no one else around them, though the beach had plenty of people on it. Still, not close enough to see anything. "Kiss me, Lukas."

"Yes." Slipping his hand up her ribcage, he dipped forward to catch her lips. She met his tongue eagerly, and shivered when his fingers inched upward to curl around her breast.

The taste of him was minty toothpaste and coffee and Lukas. She had to kick her legs to stay afloat, but she wanted to wrap them around his lean hips. Her heart pounded, and need roared through her. When his fingers dipped into her bikini top and stroked over her nipple, she shuddered, her body arching into his. She knotted her fingers in his hair, and kissed him fiercely. Suddenly, the cool water was a delightful contrast to her boiling hot flesh.

High-pitched laughter ripped her back to the present. It was a strange déjà vu from the night before. Her lips left his as she turned to look toward the pier. The same group of tween girls stood there, hands covering their mouths, eyes wide.

Incredulousness filled Lukas's voice. "Are those the same—"

"Yep." Julie snorted on a laugh and held him tighter. He chuckled with her and the next thing she knew, they'd been engulfed by the next wave of water. She came up sputtering and only laughed harder.

He shook the water from his hair, and drew her close again. "Those kids are the bane of my existence."

She nodded, arching a brow. "I found out this morning they're on the same floor I am."

The tips of his fingers ran down her sides. "You remembered what they looked like? All I remembered was the interruption."

"Nope, but they remembered me." She offered a rueful look. "The giggles were unmistakable. Fortunately, I don't think they're old enough to understand what it meant that I was wearing the same clothes as last night, or it would have been a walk of shame too."

"I'm going to have nightmares about them."

She chortled and popped a kiss on his mouth. "So, shower and figure out how to get downtown?"

"Sex in the shower first?" A hopeful lilt filled his voice and he pulled her tighter to him, so that his erection was more than obvious. Want pulsed through her, and her sex contracted on nothingness.

"I think we can arrange that." She grinned, letting her head fall back. Her grin widened when he brushed a kiss over her throat.

In under twenty-four hours, everything seemed to have changed. She'd come here looking for an escape from her life, her grief, her memories. Looking for perspective and closure. Maybe she hadn't found all of that—at least not yet—but she was smiling, laughing, having a good time. She hadn't felt this *free* since the hospital had called her with the news that Eloise had had her first stroke.

She'd spent the last year thinking about how much she hated change, how much it hurt, but Hawaii had definitely brought some good changes. Maybe they were temporary, but she'd take what she could get.

CHaPTer FIVe

"T his traffic is *awful*." Julie frowned, her voice fretful. "We'll never make it to the palace in time for our tour. Maybe you should have made the reservation for later."

Something in her tone made Lukas's muscles tighten in automatic reflex. He shook himself. Not every woman was like Lilith. Five years after the divorce and he still had to remind himself of that. Then again, he'd had seven years of conditioning before he'd finally called it quits. His ex liked to be on top of every detail. So did he, but he knew when and how to be flexible. She hadn't. If he were with Lilith right now, he'd be in for a tirade. The whining would escalate and *bam*, the world would be ending because of a traffic jam. And somehow, it would all be his fault. Because he should have made the tour reservations for later.

The bus continued to inch forward, and he made a non-committal noise. It seemed the safest response after Julie's comment.

She bumped her shoulder into his. "Well, if we miss it, maybe we'll get lucky and the next tour will have openings. Fingers crossed."

Holding up her hand, she demonstrated the overlapping fingers. He glanced at her from the corner of his eye. Again, she seemed much more laid back than he anticipated. She looped her arm through his and swiveled her head around to watch the buildings and people that passed by. Not a glimmer of distress showed on her countenance. Yeah, he really needed to stop assuming that any woman he was attracted to would eventually melt down on him. But old habits died hard and his ex had trained him far too well to expect the worst and not even bother to hope for the best.

He blew out a breath, forcing those thoughts down. It was rare for him to think about Lilith, but she'd cropped up more than once in the last day. Maybe because Julie was the woman he'd been most attracted to since his ex, which was disturbing to realize, but attraction did not equal anything more serious than that.

An older man sitting across the aisle from them looked up from his newspaper. "Where you guys trying to go?"

"The Iolani Palace," Julie answered.

"Oh, yeah. I went there on a field trip when I was a kid." The man smiled, revealing a gap-toothed grin. "Mostly it's for the *haole* tourists."

"We're definitely tourists, you're right about that." Julie dimpled.

"Where you guys from?" the man asked, folding up his newspaper.

Lukas gave a neutral shrug. He'd never felt the need to share personal information with strangers. First, it could be dangerous, depending on who the person was. Second, if you answered one question, people often felt free to ask more invasive questions, which he wasn't interested in answering. His private life was private.

"We're from California. The Bay Area." Julie shifted her purse onto her lap. "I take it you're from here, originally?"

"Me? Oh, yeah." The old man patted his chest with pride. "*Kanaka Maoli*. Pure Hawaiian."

Julie looked a little uncertain about how to respond to that. "Congratulations?"

He nodded. "You know the palace isn't that far from here."

"Really?" Julie dug around in her handbag, pulled out a map, and opened it up. She pushed one end of it toward Lukas. "Hold this, please."

Taking his end, Lukas helped her spread out the accordion-folded paper. They were silent for a few minutes as they studied.

She tapped two spots on the map. "We're here and we need to get here."

"Right." He set his finger on a spot a short distance from where they were now gridlocked on Ala Moana Boulevard. "You know, if we get off at the next stop, it's not *that* long of a walk."

"Yay, perfect!" She popped a kiss on his cheek, reached up to yank the cord to signal they wanted a stop, and then bounced out of her seat. "Let's make a run for it."

"Have fun," the old man said, and Julie gave him a parting wave. Lukas dipped his chin in acknowledgement but didn't say anything.

Ten minutes later, they still hadn't made the twenty feet to the next stop. Lukas followed Julie as she worked her way up to the front of the crowded bus, squeezing between people and dodging feet that stuck out in the aisle. When she got to the driver, she offered up a luminous smile that made Lukas's chest tighten. The woman was captivating.

"Hi," she addressed the bus driver. "We have an appointment and we'd like to get off at the next stop. Would you mind just letting us off here? We can walk."

The grizzled man looked like he was going to protest, but he glanced at Julie as her smile brightened. Lukas saw the moment the man gave in. Ducking his head, the driver pushed the lever that opened the door. "Go on."

"Thank you so much!" She clapped her hands in pleasure.

Lukas suppressed a chuckle. It seemed no one was immune to Julie's brand of charm. He certainly wasn't. So far, all she'd had to do was grin and look at him with those big brown eyes and he was toast.

They stepped off the bus into the balmy air. She cast him a quick glance. "For the record, you're going to need to lead the way. My sense of direction is atrocious, and we don't have time to get lost. Should I get the map out again?"

"No, I've got it up here." He tapped a finger against his temple. "This way."

"Oh, thank God." She scurried to keep up with his longer stride as they took off down the street and passed the bus. "If both of us sucked with directions, we'd have been so hosed."

He shook his head and grinned. He liked that she had a good sense of humor about her flaws. Sure, it could be an act, but everything about Julie had appeared genuine thus far. Being upfront about her issue with navigation meant they could work around it rather than ignore it. Her attitude was refreshing. He had far too many colleagues with more ego than good sense, and God forbid they should ever admit they didn't know everything.

They wove through the streets of downtown until they got to South King Street and turned left. On one side was the courthouse and on the other was the palace. They paused for a moment when they reached the front gate and gazed at the massive gray structure. Slender columns held up two stories of verandahs in the front, squares towers occupied each corner, and a wide drive lined with manicured lawns led up from the green and gold gates.

Julie tilted her head. "Wow, that's even prettier than in the picture on the website."

A glance at his watch showed Lukas they really needed to hurry. He started tugging her forward.

"We need to head to the barracks to check in for our tour." He pointed to a building off to the side. "We're a little late, but hopefully they haven't started without us."

"Let's make a run for it." With that, she surprised him by abandoning all pretense of dignity and dashing down the drive.

What surprised him even more was that he went along and raced her to the barracks. Not his normal behavior, but it was fun. He grabbed her around the waist just as they reached the building, spun her around, and kissed her. Just because he could. Just because it felt good.

T hey made it in time for their tour. Just barely, but they made it. Now they were with a group of other visitors waiting for the guides to take them inside. They sat in rows of wooden benches on the palace's back porch and put ugly cotton footies over their shoes so they didn't damage the floor. It made sense, but still, they looked ridiculous.

She positioned her swathed feet next to Lukas's, snapped a picture, and texted it to her friends with the caption: *About to take a tour of the Iolani Palace. Check out the required footwear!*

Karen sent back, *Stylish!*

Anne's text came in next. *It's a foot condom!*

Another ten seconds passed before Meg answered. *Wait, whose feet are those next to yours?*

Busted. Julie hadn't even been thinking when she photographed her feet next to his. It had just been a nice visual. She quickly replied, *Time to go on the tour. Talk to you later!*

With that, she shut off her phone and stuffed it into her purse.

There were going to be some entertaining messages when she finally checked it again, but she wasn't having that confession session in front of Lukas. Men never understood the female need to share everything with their girlfriends, so she had always thought it best to go by the old saying, "What they don't know won't hurt them." She huffed a laugh. Anne would demand voyeuristically salacious details—mostly just to yank Julie's chain—which wouldn't happen, so it wasn't as if she was really planning to tell her friends *everything*.

Lukas glanced at her. "What's funny?"

"My friends. I sent them a picture of the footies." She paddled her foot condoms through the air.

He hummed and nodded. "They're quite classy."

"Exactly."

The docent broke into their conversation. "If you'll all follow me, please."

Lukas took her hand as they stood, and she twined her fingers with his. It was nice. This whole morning had been nice. Probably the first time she *hadn't* thought about Auntie Eloise upon waking. Then again, not anticipating going into her late aunt's shop might have helped, but Julie had woken with a smile on her face that had everything to do with getting laid.

Allowing Lukas to pull her along, she stepped into the former home of Hawaiian royalty. The sweep of the carved koa wood staircase caught her attention immediately and she hauled Lukas over to look.

It was a gorgeous house. Not as massive as some of the palaces in Europe, but every bit as beautiful. The room where they'd imprisoned the queen made Julie sad. Sure, the lady hadn't been abused, but a nice cage was still a cage. What a terrible thing, to have your country taken away.

In the basement, there were displays of the royal jewels as well as information on Hawaiian history, including one of the islands' time as a leper colony. Equal parts lovely and horrifying. When they emerged an hour later, she had a much deeper respect for the islands than before she'd arrived. Which had been the point, she supposed.

Lukas squeezed her hand. "Beautiful, isn't it?"

"Yes." She glanced back at the imposing gray building. "It really is."

They strolled along the path between wide green lawns, heading toward the gate by the converted barracks where they'd bought their tickets. The humidity wrapped around them, and she thought they might be in for another rain shower. If it was as short as the one yesterday, it would be no big deal. They could duck into a coffee shop or something and wait it out.

Once they were out on the street, Lukas tugged her to the right. "Did you want to check out Chinatown? It's not terribly far from here."

She followed along without protest. Making it downtown hadn't been high on her to-do list, but they were here, so why not explore? "Would this be your first time to Chinatown, too?"

"Yep. I've never managed to come anywhere near this area of Honolulu." He looked both ways, then led her across the road and up Hotel Street. "Call me crazy, but I'm betting they have Chinese food in Chinatown. Want to grab lunch there?"

Since she hadn't had more than a granola bar for breakfast, her stomach rumbled an emphatic affirmative. "Sounds good. I would kill for a good egg roll right now."

He winked at her. "Well, let's get you fed before something dangerous and homicidal happens."

"Smart man." She swung their linked arms between them, looking around to see everything as they went by.

They passed a mall, the business district, and a few statues before they reached the neighborhood they wanted. Chinatown turned out to be a mishmash of Asian cultures, with a Vietnamese pharmacy next to a Thai grocery store. They skipped over a few restaurants that seemed a little dim and seedy. It wasn't the most affluent area, though she didn't feel unsafe. Of course, that might be partly because of the six-foot tall man at her side. Funny what a difference that could make.

"Hey, what's that?" They got to what appeared to be a general store, though the signs were all in an Asian language she couldn't recognize. Sitting in wooden bins outside were fruits and vegetables of varieties she'd never seen before. The one she had pointed at was bright red with green spikes.

Lukas narrowed his eyes at it. "I *think* it's called a dragon fruit, but I'm not sure."

"Huh. Should we buy one and try it?" She leaned closer to inspect one of the fruits. Would it be as red on the inside as it was on the outside? Or green like the spikes? What would the thing taste like?

"Mmm, I wouldn't." He tugged her hand to get her started down the street again. "First, we don't know for sure *what* it is, which means we don't know whether it's ripe or of good quality or not. Second, we don't know if you can eat it raw or if you have to cook it. I don't have any way to cook something in my hotel room. Do you?"

"No." She shrugged. "Those are all good points, too. I'll look dragon fruit up when we get back, just so I can see if that really is one."

"Sounds like a plan." He grinned, laughter lurking in his gaze.

She arched her brows. "What?"

One broad shoulder rolled in an easy shrug. "Just enjoying you enjoying everything around you."

Blinking, she cocked her head. "Well, I enjoy you. Especially last night."

The grin turned positively sinful and hot enough to melt the panties off any woman alive. His thumb rubbed sensuous circles in the middle of her palm. "I hope you enjoy me again. Repeatedly. When I'm well-rested, I'm good for more than just one round."

All the air rushed out of her lungs, and the desire that always seemed to be just below the surface with them sizzled to life. Her tongue stuck to the roof of her mouth when he brought her hand to his lips and bit the tip of her index finger, then kissed away the sting.

"So...lunch?" He lifted one eyebrow as if he hadn't just left her a quivering mass of want.

She shook herself out of her stupor. "I'm going to pay you back for that later."

"I look forward to it."

A shiver went through her at the many ideas of how she could exact her revenge. Maybe sucking him until he was ready to come and then backing off. Or kissing, licking, and biting her way from one end of him to the other. Oh yeah. She would love to make him beg.

Okay, she had to stop thinking about that or she was going to implode right there in the middle of Honolulu. Holy God, the man lit her on fire with a single look. She'd never had that happen before, and it was fabulous.

"What about this one?" Lukas stopped in front of a place with handwritten menus hanging on the wall. The items available were written in both English and a Chinese dialect. At least, she thought it was Chinese.

They stepped inside. One side of the room was dominated by a huge glass bakery case, and the other side held tables and chairs for customers.

Standing in silence, they read over the food choices. Then she leaned toward him. "Does that really say pig blood rice soup?"

"Yes, it does." He tapped a fingertip against his chin. "Would that be better or worse than squid?"

"I think that's an experiment best left unconducted, Doctor," she retorted with a shudder. There was a limit to the new experiences she wanted on this trip. Eating anything with *blood* in the title was definitely over the line. "The Singapore rice noodles sound much more edible—I mean, appetizing."

"Freudian slip?" He ruffled her hair and she stuck her tongue out at him in return. "So, you're okay with this place?"

"Let's find a table." She turned on her phone to get a picture of the menu, noting that she had several missed messages from her friends. They'd have to wait. She snapped a photo, switched her phone to silent and stuffed it in her purse.

A waitress with a thick accent came along to take their orders, then disappeared into the back. Within fifteen minutes, they had their food. It was tasty and the place was quiet. Rain had begun pattering against the street outside, and Julie was glad to be inside. No need to rush the meal. They were the only customers in the place, but that might have been due to the weather.

"How are the Shanghai noodles?" he asked.

"Singapore. They're good." She forked up a generous portion and held it out to him. "Try some."

His strong fingers wrapped around her wrist and guided her hand to his mouth. He took the food, but his gaze locked with hers. Fire flashed in those blue depths, and a quiver settled low in her belly. She wanted him. Now. Again. And there wasn't a thing she could do about it, since they were miles from their hotel. His lips quirked in a half-grin as he released her hand, chewing the bite she'd given him.

"Delicious. Want some of mine?" The innuendo in his question was unmistakable.

Words failed her. He was trying to kill her, he really was. If he weren't sitting across the table from her, she might not have been able to keep her hands to herself. She swallowed, cleared her throat, and just as she was about to say something, the restaurant's door opened and a few more customers spilled in.

With the addition of other people, Julie and Lukas settled into more mundane conversation. He wanted to know more about her business and the crafts she specialized in. She found out more about his research. It occurred to her while they ate that he was exactly the kind of man she'd love to date back home. Which was sad because she had a gut feeling that he wouldn't be interested in the same. Not that he wasn't interested in *her*, per se, but that relationships weren't even on his radar. There was a certain attitude about a man who was open to a relationship, and Lukas didn't give off that vibe at all. He wanted a vacation fling, and nothing more.

Then again, when she'd arrived the day before, she hadn't exactly been in a headspace where a relationship was even close to something she'd consider. Maybe it was better not to let her thoughts stray in that direction, and just have fun with Lukas in the days they had left. She wouldn't mind spending more time with him like they'd done yesterday and today. Not just in bed, but hanging out, talking, getting to know each other, and seeing the sights together.

Maybe that made this a mini-relationship. All the good parts with none of the bad. It would be over too soon to get her heart trampled, but she got a few days to remember how fun it could be to have a boyfriend. Or something. Maybe it was best not to dwell on it. Embrace the moment, the way Eloise would have done. Yeah, that was the best idea.

The waitress came out bearing a huge baking pan loaded with golden brown rolls. "Hong Kong bun, fresh from oven. You want for dessert?" She brought the pan closer to Julie and Lukas's table, so a whiff of heavenly scent filled her nose. The waitress grinned. "Sweet coconut butter in center. Very good. You want some?"

"Yes," Julie and Lukas said at the same time.

Julie laughed. "I'm stuffed but it looks so *good*. I just have to try one."

Their server set the pan down on the empty table next to theirs, went to grab two plates and a spatula, and dished their dessert right in front of them.

Lukas quirked a brow as the waitress took the pan away to the bakery counter. "That woman knows how to advertise. No one could have resisted."

In answer, Julie moaned as she took her first bite. "Oh my God, they taste even better than they look. The coconut butter filling is *amazing*."

His gaze was glued to her mouth, hunger that had nothing to do with food reflecting back at her. "Julie."

Since he'd teased her multiple times today, she figured she should play this up. She chewed another bite, savoring slowly. She threw in another moan for good measure. "So. Yummy." Then she echoed his earlier words. "Want some?"

He cleared his throat, a bite of his bun suspended halfway to his mouth. "Did you want to head back to the hotel after this?"

The roughness in his voice went straight to her core, making her body throb. "Yes."

"Let's pray the traffic has cleared up."

"Ugh. *Traffic*." There was a real killjoy. If the roads were clear, it would take about twenty minutes to get back. If they weren't clear, the wait until she could jump Lukas's bones was indefinite. Patience might be a virtue, but she'd never claimed to be virtuous. If she were, she wouldn't be shagging a virtual stranger.

"It would be worth the wait." His gaze dipped down to caress her breasts, and she felt her nipples tighten.

She hurried her way through dessert. As good as it was, it couldn't even begin to compete with how good Lukas was. Delicious. And half the calories.

T hey maintained a casual pace from the bus stop to her hotel room, but it was a sham. There was nothing casual going on. The way she'd been looking at him the entire ride back had made Lukas want to rip her clothes off and fuck her until she begged him for mercy.

"So, did any other Stanford professors go to your conference?" Her palm grazed his ass as they walked through the lobby, though her expression was one of pure innocence, the little witch.

He shook his head, pressed his hand to the middle of her back, lengthened his stride, and urged her to hurry. "No, though one of the two presentations I gave was about joint research I'd conducted with a couple of colleagues in my department. Terry and Sven."

"Yeah? What are Terry and Sven like?" She sounded a bit breathless as she all but jogged to keep up with him. "And is Terry a guy or a girl?"

They reached her room's tower and he stabbed the elevator call button. Trying to concentrate on a normal conversation when he wanted to have her naked and underneath him was pure torture. "Terry is a guy. He likes to do very manly things in his spare time, like shoot machine guns."

"A machine gun toting physicist?" She cocked her head and her gaze sparkled with glee. "Okay, then. Why not?"

Just as the elevator car reached the ground level, an elderly couple joined them to wait. Damn, he wasn't going to be able to get his hands on her during the ride up. He ground his teeth with impatience. It did nothing to ease his pique that the old couple looked them over with obvious curiosity. He could only hope they didn't take the opportunity to ask nosy questions.

The elevator came and all four of them boarded. Julie pushed the button for her floor, which was lower than the other pair's. Good. The sooner he had her alone, the better.

He leaned closer to Julie and said, "Sven also has a degree in electrical engineering and is something of an expert on the workings of the electric chair. He has an old one sitting outside his office."

The elderly duo gave him a startled look and edged away a little. It amused him more than it probably should have. Academics were rarely considered terrifying, except to their students and junior colleagues.

Julie made a face. "That's kind of creepy."

"That's Sven."

She cast him a glance out of the corner of her eye. "It sounds like a Scandinavian name."

"It is." He was already grinning in anticipation of her response.

"Hmm." She lifted an eyebrow. "My theory about creepy Scandinavians is still holding."

"So it seems." The elevator pinged as they reached the right floor and he stepped out just behind Julie.

She slipped her card key from her purse and had her door open in seconds. He locked it behind them, then turned on her like a tiger on its prey. She tossed her purse aside and silently began stripping off her clothes. He did the same, and there was fire in her gaze as he unzipped his pants that made his erection strain against his boxers. Her enticing curves came into view, breasts just large enough to fill his palms tipped with dusky brown nipples. A slender waist flared out into rounded hips and the most amazing ass he'd ever seen in his life. Her legs were long and slender and made for being wrapped around a man's waist. The thought made his sex throb.

When they were naked, she moved into his embrace, those soft breasts pillowed against him and her tight little nipples stabbed into his chest. Her gaze met his for a long, protracted moment. Then they fell on each other like wild animals. A part of Lukas told him to slow down, to take care not to hurt her, but her hands cupped his erection and her mouth was fused with his. She bit his tongue and he growled in response, his control shredding to nothing.

He pulled back and spun her toward the bed. He needed her *now*. She landed on the mattress on her hands and knees, providing him with an unobstructed view of the luscious curve of her backside and the slick lips of her sex. Before he did something stupid, like plunge himself into her without another thought, he reached for his pants and the protection he had tucked in his wallet.

His hands shook as he sheathed himself in a condom. He knelt on the bed behind her and, grasping his shaft, rubbed the head up and down her slit before he eased himself into her tight, wet heat. One long steady push and he was hilted within her. He pressed a hand to the small of her back, groaning at how good she felt.

He reached around her to cup her breasts and roll her nipples between his fingers. A mewling little cry burst from her, and she shoved her hips back against his groin. They both groaned as her movement drove him deeper into her sex. He tried to go slowly, tried to wring every last ounce of pleasure out of the experience, but instead he pounded inside her. Faster, harder. He'd never lost his self-restraint so quickly, but she was right there with him, matching his movements, moaning her encouragement.

She folded her arms to the side and her shoulders and head dropped to the mattress. The angle made her channel clamp tighter on his shaft with each thrust, and he gripped her hips hard enough he feared he'd leave bruises. But holy shit, that was amazing. If the sensation were any more intense, his skull might explode.

He thrust deep, withdrew. After slipping one hand around her, he delved into the thatch of hair between her thighs, flicking his thumb over her nub. He smoothed his other palm in circles over her hip and down to her backside. The feel of her silky skin was perfect, and he drew back his hand to smack the round globe of her backside. She squeaked in surprise, jolting forward, but that just pressed her against his stroking fingers.

Her back bowed, a shiver rippling through her. He watched goose bumps break down her skin. "Faster, Lukas. Harder. *Please.*"

He had no problem complying with that request. He bucked his hips, slamming into her again and again. He continued toying with her wet flesh, loving the sounds of pleasure that broke from her throat. Sweat slid down his skin and his muscles burned from the speed of his movements. "Do you have any idea how it feels to be inside you?"

"Do you have any idea how it feels to have you inside me?" She squeezed her inner muscles around him. "I think I'm getting the better end of this deal, frankly."

He laughed and plunged into her slick channel. When was the last time he'd laughed during sex? Her giggle warmed his insides, but he didn't have the mental capacity left to consider why. All that existed now was the drive to completion. The grip of her sleek sex told him just how close she was to orgasm. He wanted to send her flying into oblivion. He ground his pelvis into her backside and flicked a finger against her nub. Hard.

She cried out, her hips snapping back to meet his thrusts. "Oh my

God, *Lukas!*"

The sensation of her channel flexing around his length was more than enough to spin him over into his own orgasm. "Julie!"

Fluids exploded from him, the rush so incredible he wasn't sure of his own name when it was done. All he heard was the low, husky sound of her chuckle. "Lukas, my friend, that was hot. You can do that to me any time."

He patted her butt. "Give me half an hour, and I'll take you up on that offer."

"Mmm." She stretched against the mattress, making little sounds of contented satisfaction. "I'd like to spend the rest of the day in bed."

And that was exactly what they did. Making love, napping in each other's arms, then waking up to do it all over again. It was passion fueled by fire hot enough to melt. For dinner, rather than leave the room, Lukas ordered a pizza delivery from the parlor in the hotel's shopping village. He didn't want to do anything to disturb the mood of the day. This was as close to perfection as he'd ever been.

They sat cross-legged on the mattress, eating slices of pepperoni from paper plates. Her cheeks were still flushed from their last round of sex, her lips swollen from his kisses. She wore nothing but his shirt, and it was a powerful aphrodisiac to watch her—her smooth skin shone in the fading sunlight that spilled through the window, her dark hair tussled. She darted her tongue out to catch a drop of marinara that lingered at the corner of her mouth.

"We missed the sunset on the beach today." Her lips formed an exaggerated pout.

"That is a shame." He set aside his plate. "Swimming tomorrow?"

She shook her head. "Nope, I have to rise and shine early to pick up the rental car. Pearl Harbor, remember? I hear the North Shore is spectacular, so I also wanted to drive around the island." She waved a vague hand toward the desk, which was cluttered with books, folded maps, and paperwork. "The guidebook says it's easy to do in a day."

"It is." He wiped his mouth with a napkin. "The Hawaiian Islands aren't very big."

Her glance was a little shy. "I had fun today."

"Me, too." Probably more fun than it was healthy to have.

She bit her lower lip. "Do you want to come with me? As long as I drive, I don't think it ups the rental fee to have another person in the car."

"Yes." The agreement was out of his mouth before he had a chance to consider it. He wanted to spend all the time he had with her. There wasn't a thing about her that he didn't like. The way she made him feel, made him laugh, turned him inside out was starting to become a bit worrying. He *reacted* when he was around her, instead of carefully mulling over his options the way he normally did. Emotional responses weren't his forte—in fact, that was one of the things he liked about science. It was rational, logical. It had rules that made sense, unlike most women. Feeling instead of thinking wasn't a response he liked to have, ever, but especially when it came to the female half of the population.

He'd thought Julie was dangerous the day he'd met her, and their time together since had only proven how right he was. Only the fact that this *thing* they had going was deadline-specific kept him from breaking into a cold sweat.

CHAPTER SIX

"This car is ridiculous. It looks like a purple bubble." Julie patted the wheel as she pulled up to the stop sign outside the rental company. After looking both ways, she turned the corner onto the next street. The morning had dawned breezy and beautiful, and she was more than a little excited about the adventure they were going on. This was the only part of her trip that she'd planned for, and having Lukas along made it even better.

He smirked. "Well, they probably get discounts on buying the ugly cars from dealers. You got the car so ugly only its mother could love it."

It took a lot of effort for her to keep a straight face. "Aw, it's not *ugly*...it's just different."

"'It looks like a purple bubble,'" he quoted, doing a remarkably accurate impression of her voice.

She reached over and poked him in the side, which made him break into a spasm of laughter. "Uh oh. Someone's *ticklish*."

He fended her off with a hand. "None of that, Julie. You're driving. Watch the road."

"Spoilsport," she shot back, but did as he asked and focused on driving.

It turned out that Lukas was an excellent navigator. He'd pulled up a map on his phone and had directions ready to go, despite the fact that she'd printed out directions and brought them with her. Even when she missed their exit off the freeway, he stayed calm and quickly found an alternate route. His steadiness was reassuring while traversing unfamiliar roads.

She would have been fine on her own, would have figured things out, but it was nice having him along. She was glad she'd asked him. It occurred to her that she might be spending her entire vacation with him, and the idea didn't bother her in the least. She'd gone with him for his downtown excursion yesterday and now, here he was on her circumnavigation of the island. She hadn't expected to have company when she came here, but she wasn't going to complain about it either. Lukas was rock solid and had been a pretty fantastic problem solver when issues cropped up. Not a bad companion to have.

And that was without factoring in his skills in the bedroom. Those alone would be worth keeping him around for the trip, even if he was a drag outside of the sack. Well, maybe she'd be less gung-ho to spend time with him, but he'd have been an excellent booty call every night.

They made it to Pearl Harbor in good time, and the memorial was far more extensive than she'd realized. There were multiple buildings with exhibits on the shore before they even took their turn on the ferry out to the white monument that straddled the sunken remains of the *USS Arizona*.

She stood arm in arm with Lukas as they stared out over the water. They could see the full breadth of the ship, and she shuddered to think of all the people who'd died there. People who were far too young. Julie hated to consider what their families had felt like when they received the news. So many lives, over just like that.

It occurred to her that if they'd been back in 1941, she and Lukas would have been enemies. American and German. Opposite sides of an awful war. Somehow it felt right to commemorate this place with a man like him. He took pictures of the oil, which still leaked from the ship and turned the water into a liquid rainbow, while she went to explore the rest of the monument.

Tears gathered in her eyes as she read the list of names carved in a marble wall at one end of the memorial. All those who'd lost their lives. There was black tape over one name, and it took her a moment to realize that it was someone who had survived the attack, but had recently died and was being added to the list. The man would have been around the same age as Auntie Eloise. Unlike the young men who'd died during the attack, they'd lived to a ripe old age.

That was one thing she didn't have to lament with Eloise—while her loss had been sudden, Eloise's death had been a natural one, brought on by old age. This memorial and the enormity of what had happened here put some of Julie's personal loss into perspective, which was both sad and helpful at the same time. Her great-aunt could have died young, and then Julie would never have had a chance to know her. Or she could have had less time with her. Losing her hurt, but it might have been so much worse. The years they'd had together were precious, and Julie needed to focus on that instead of wishing she could have had more.

The loss was bittersweet and always would be, but for the first time, it was more sweet than bitter. A good change, if a small one. She'd take it.

Several hours later, Lukas walked beside her as they left the gift shop. She had postcards for her friends and a magnet to put on her fridge. Lukas had a book about the attack on Pearl Harbor. He wrapped an arm around her as they walked out to the parking lot. "You're quiet."

She nodded. "It's really peaceful here. Still, it feels...sad."

He squeezed her closer to his side. "Places that commemorate tragedy often do. There are several war memorials in Europe with the same peaceful sadness. I suppose it encourages reflection."

"About how not to do that again. 'Those who don't learn from history are doomed to repeat it,' and all that." After pulling the rental keys out of her purse, she popped open the car's doors.

"Exactly." He opened her door for her, then looped around to settle in the passenger seat. "Let's hope that bit of history is never repeated."

They sat for a few minutes in a pool of silence. She wasn't sure what he was thinking about, but she doubted the monument had affected him as profoundly as it had her. She took a deep breath. "Okay, which way to the North Shore?"

"Right." He sat up a little straighter and dug his phone out of his pocket. "We'll continue along the 99, then hop over to the 2, then switch over to the 80 for a shortcut back to the 99, and then—" He paused to look at her when she made a sound of dismay. His gaze went from her to the map. "Um, why don't I just tell you when to be ready for a turn?"

"Perfect." She put the key in the ignition and within a few minutes they were back on the road.

Lukas pointed to something on his phone. "How do you feel about stopping for a pineapple float at the Dole Plantation? We're going to drive right by it."

She blinked. "I've never even heard of a pineapple float."

"Pineapple juice with pineapple ice cream. You have no idea what you're missing. It's amazing." His face creased in a boyish grin. "They also have a miniature train that goes around the plantation."

"Well, we can't miss that." She signaled to merge onto the 99. "Besides, I bet they have postcards for me to send back to the mainland."

"There's only one way to find out."

They climbed back into the car two hours later, and Lukas felt a little queasy from the amount of ice cream and pineapple juice he'd consumed. It had been too good to stop, which seemed to be his excuse for indulging in everything on this trip. He pushed that unwelcome realization aside and shut the passenger side door behind him. The car was almost too compact for someone of his height to find comfortable, but he managed. It meant that every time they went around a corner, he swayed into Julie and their shoulders brushed. The intimacy of it felt strange and comforting at the same time. He wasn't sure what to make of that feeling, so he ignored it to focus on his companion.

"That was delish." Julie smacked her lips and flipped on the blinker to go left. "We should maybe find some lunch soon to make up for the sugar, though."

"Right," Lukas said. "I mean, you need to *turn* right."

"Ah." She flushed, gave a bashful little shrug, and set the blinker to signal a right turn. "My bad."

"No problem. You just wanted to take the scenic route." He reached over to tug on a lock of her hair.

"Yeah." She chuckled. "Only the North Shore is supposed to be one of the most scenic routes in the world, so maybe we should stick with our original plan."

He watched her pull the car back out on the highway, relaxing into his seat. He couldn't get enough of how much she relished everything.

He'd never met anyone quite like her. She wasn't saccharine or obnoxiously cheerful—she was just having a good time. Someone like her seemed too good to be true. Other than her nonexistent sense of direction, she was a delight.

But he'd seen moments in the last couple of days when she lost a bit of the sparkle in her eyes. He wanted to ask her about it, but wasn't sure he should pry, since those kinds of questions usually annoyed him. Hypocrisy wasn't his thing, so he had to guess at why she might be sad. Perhaps it was spending the holidays without her friends and family, and perhaps not. Perhaps it was only about her deceased great-aunt. How much did he really know about her? Less than he wanted to, which was one more reason to keep his mouth shut. He felt too much when she was around, and emotions weren't to be trusted.

He cleared his throat. "There are a few restaurants on the way. So we can have some sustenance to go with our early dessert."

"Sweet. Or rather, savory."

He snorted and propped his elbow on the window ledge. After about a mile, she reached across the console and took his other hand to twine her fingers with his. He gave her a slight squeeze and watched the scenery roll by. Mostly agricultural fields, without a hint of the ocean that was always so nearby.

"We're going to come up on a fork in the road soon. You want to go right." He pointed to emphasize. "The 83 will take us around the North Shore."

"Got it." She shot him a chagrined look. "Even I can follow those directions."

"You're not that bad." Only he had no idea how bad she really was. He'd been navigating on this trip and the one downtown yesterday.

She snorted. "You know how we met at the convention center?"

"Of course." He doubted he'd ever forget the first time he saw her, even years after they'd parted ways. Not that he needed to acknowledge that to anyone but himself.

"Yeah, I wasn't there just to get out of the rain." Her nose wrinkled. "I got lost trying to get back to the Hilton from the mall."

He tried to turn a laugh into a cough, but doubted he was very convincing. "Um. You just stay on Ala Moana and you're right there."

"Sounds easy, doesn't it? I came in that way, and it seemed like a pretty straight shot, but I ended up getting turned around inside the mall, left through a different entrance than I came in, and then couldn't *find* Ala Moana."

Compressing his lips, he nodded. "Yeah, you really are that bad."

She released his hand to wave hers through the air. "I print out maps to everything. Seriously, everything. When I first moved to San Francisco...it was bad. That's all I can say. There's all these hills and winding roads and the architecture is all pretty similar. I had a purse full of maps to all the places I normally go. Work, the grocery store, the library. I never moved once I settled because I wasn't sure I'd ever figure out how to get places from a different direction."

"Ouch," he commiserated. While it probably led to hilarious bloopers, he imagined a problem like that would be a pain in the ass to live with.

"I know, right?" She shrugged. "At least being back in Half Moon Bay has the advantage that I lived there for eighteen years, so I know my way around."

They came to the fork in the road and Julie made the correct turn without further prompting. The ocean loomed to the left and waves crashed on the shore. Cars lined both sides of the road and surfers dotted the swells, riding the breakers. Fortunately, most of the other drivers went slowly, so Lukas and Julie got a good look at the sparkling blue surf. It was beyond picturesque.

The car jolted and shuddered, swerving slightly.

"Oh shit." Julie's face went pale. She braked to a stop and pulled the car over into a sandy spot on the side of the road.

Lukas clutched at his armrest but tried to keep his voice calm. "I'm guessing we blew a tire."

"That's what it sounded like to me." She glanced over her shoulder and waited for traffic to clear enough to let her open the door. "Okay, let's see if this thing has a spare."

Lukas hopped out and met her at the back of the car. "A lug wrench and jack would be welcome too."

They stared at the flatter-than-a-pancake rear passenger tire. A long nail stuck out of the tread at the top. Lukas squatted down and pressed his fingertip against the nail's head. "Well, that answers that."

"Damn." Julie bent until she could get a good look at it. She blew out a breath, a frown snapping her brows together. "That is one flat tire, and trying to change it on sandy soil is going to suck ass. Doing it in a dress is going to suck even more. Blech."

He rose and stepped back, his normal wariness when confronted with an upset woman coming to the fore. "I can take care of it for you, if you like."

Better to handle it on his own than deal with her getting livid over things they had no control over. They weren't going anywhere on that wheel, and the packed roadways meant it could be miles before they found somewhere else to park. They were lucky to have made it to this spot.

"Nah. I know how to change a tire." She tossed up a helpless hand. "You're my guest on this little jaunt. I don't want to rope you in as unpaid labor."

After moving to the trunk, she unlocked and opened the back while he gaped at her in surprise. This wasn't the first time she hadn't freaked out when plans went awry. It threw him off every time her unflappable nature surfaced. He really needed to get past that. Hell, he had a lot of things he needed to get past—most of them rooted in the catastrophe of his marriage. Being around Julie was making it more and more clear how much his divorce still affected him, how much what Lilith had done still colored his view of women. He did just fine when they were colleagues or friends, but add any kind of romantic involvement and he braced himself for every situation to go sideways.

He had to stop that. Maybe he'd never be ready for a real relationship again, but automatically casting attractive women into the role of controlling, irrational villainess wasn't the way he wanted to live. He would *not* let his ex have that much power over him. It was a revelation to consider how much power he'd already given her, even after their marriage was post-mortem.

"You okay?" Julie's words brought him back to the present. "You have a funny expression on your face."

He shook himself and found that she'd already unloaded the jack and lug wrench, and was currently wrestling with the spare. Hurrying to her side, he helped her maneuver the thing out of the trunk.

"Thanks." She tossed a wink at him. "How deep do you think the sand goes before we hit solid ground?"

"Not terribly far. We'll be okay, I think." He rolled the new tire over and dropped it near the flat one. "Let's try it. If we can't do it, we'll call a tow truck."

She picked up the jack and positioned it under the car. "I have AAA roadside assistance, so as long as we have cell reception, I have that part covered."

"Let's hope it doesn't come to that." He helped her raise the car enough to get the old tire off, but it was a pure bitch because the soil *was* half-sand. Beads of sweat slid down his temples, not just because of the exertion, but the stress that any second, the jack was going to slip.

Working together in silence, they got the new tire on in record time. He figured she was just as worried as he was about the ground giving out on them, so speed was essential. She heaved a huge sigh when they tightened the last lug nut on the spare.

He started to lower the car, and the jack finally gave up the fight against the sand and slid sideways. The tire hit ground hard and the shocks squeaked in protest. He grabbed Julie around the waist and shoved her back a step while the vehicle resettled on the new wheel. His heart pounded in his chest, a spurt of adrenaline shooting through him. "Are you all right?"

"Yeah." Her arms encircled his waist from behind, and she peered around him. "Whew. Looks like we got that done just in time."

"So it seems." He closed his eyes and sighed in relief. No harm done. Other than being a little dirty and sweaty, they were both all right, and the car was fine.

With her pressed to his back, he felt her stomach rumble and she snickered, burying her face between his shoulder blades. "Um...let's get everything stowed and find that food we wanted. My sugar high has crashed hard by now."

"A place to wash our hands would be nice too." He scooped up the popped tire and headed for the trunk, leaving her to follow with the jack and wrench.

"Well, there's a shrimp truck across the street. I see lunch in our future." She slammed the trunk closed, then went around to the passenger door and reached through to grab her purse.

He watched her pull a wet wipe out of the bag and hand it to him, then use one to swipe at the worst of the grime on her hands and arms. He did the same. Not his favorite way to clean up, but better than nothing. "Thanks. With any luck, they have somewhere to wash more thoroughly."

"Aw, you didn't have any problem being sweaty and dirty with me yesterday," she teased.

He tapped a somewhat clean finger against the tip of her nose. "*That* is an entirely different thing."

Slinging her purse strap over her shoulder, she locked the car. "We can talk dirty later. My belly button is rubbing a blister on my backbone."

He choked on a breath. "That's a colorful way to word it."

"Let's make a run for it." She tossed the keys into her bag and looped around the car to look both ways on the busy highway. The road was congested, but the cars drove slowly enough that after a few minutes, vehicles had pulled to a stop in both directions to let them cross. Julie gave both drivers a jaunty wave.

Lukas placed a hand to the middle of her back, urging her forward. "Traffic apparently waits for one woman, but lunch waits for no man."

"*Foooooood.*" She drew the word out as if it tasted good.

The scent of cooking seafood hit his nose and his stomach gave a grinding wrench of hunger. Saliva filled his mouth in anticipation. Even if the food was barely mediocre, it was going to taste like ambrosia anyway. They joined a short line of people waiting to order, and had their food in no time. Julie hadn't even settled onto a picnic bench before she dug into hers. Lukas managed to sit down first, but he chuckled at her enthusiasm.

"Man, we are scoring with the food on this trip. The Chinese food place, and now the shrimp scampi." She made a face. "Okay, the calamari incident notwithstanding."

He quirked an eyebrow. "I disagree that the calamari was anything other than an additional score to our food luck. The spicy garlic shrimp today is quite good too."

"We will agree to disagree on the squid." She lifted a hand to shield her eyes, taking in the view of the ocean from where they sat. "It really is spectacular here. I wish—"

She cut herself off, shook her head, and a crooked smile curved her lips.

There it was—the melancholy that sometimes darkened her expression. He shouldn't ask about it. He'd already decided not to, but that didn't stop the question from coming out of his mouth. He couldn't sit there and do nothing. "You wish for what?"

"Nothing. Don't worry about it." She stuffed a bite of food into her mouth.

"You seem sad." He caught her hand over the table. "Off and on for the last few days, I see these moments in your eyes where you look terribly lost and...sad."

Reluctance shone in her gaze. She tucked her shoulder into her chin in an awkward shrug. "I've been feeling lost and sad for the last year. My great-aunt would have loved it here. She would have hit on some of the retired men. And some of the young single ones. She'd have loved the band that first night, the palace, the Chinese food place, Pearl Harbor, the North Shore. All of it. I wish I could share it with her, but I can't because she's *dead*. It's gotten easier as the months have passed, but every now and then it just hits me. Wham. And I'm right back to that grieving place."

He rubbed his thumb over her knuckles, a knot of sympathy forming in his chest. "I'm sorry."

She nodded and kept her gaze on her plate. "It's even worse than it was with my mom. Maybe because I was closer to Eloise than Mom, maybe because I had Eloise longer. Maybe because when Mom passed, I still had Eloise, so I didn't feel quite so orphaned." She blew out a breath. "I'm doing better, I really am. I *know* how lucky I am to have had them in my life and I'm so grateful that I got to keep them as long as I did. But with my great-aunt...it's just *hard* to lose someone who seemed so larger than life, so invincible."

"She sounds like an amazing woman." He reached out and caught her chin, lifting it until she looked at him. "I can see where you take after her."

"That's kind. Thank you." Disbelief and flattery reflected in her eyes. "Eloise left some very big shoes to fill though. I'm not sure I have quite the *joie de vivre* that she did."

"I think you do." He released her chin. "There aren't many people I've met who manage to make fun out of nothing the way you can. And so far, you've been pretty bombproof, no matter what happens."

He hoped she believed that, because he knew how hard it was to dig out from under the grief when a loved one died. It took a long time and the pain never went away entirely—it just got easier to bear. Julie was doing better than she thought she was, and in his opinion, her view on life was to credit for that. A view she seemed to have inherited from her great-aunt.

"Thanks. Really...thanks." She flushed and bit her lip. "I've...uh...never told anyone about losing Eloise being worse than losing my mom. I've always felt kind of guilty about it, like I should have loved my mom best. But she and I were pretty different. We loved each other and she was awesome—both of my parents were—but when there's no common ground it's hard to have a deep connection."

"Family dynamics are complicated, Julie. Don't feel bad about that." He leaned forward. "The important part is that you all loved each other."

That lopsided grin formed on her face again. "You're right. Mom was the ultimate sportswoman, and *loved* to go hunting and fishing with my dad. I always opted to stay with Eloise. We'd sit in her shop, knit, and gossip with her customers. And every now and then, she'd just hop in the car with me and go for a drive. She liked seeing places she'd never been." A laugh straggled out of her, and tears glistened in her eyes before she blinked them away. "One time, we went to Lake Tahoe for lunch. Just because."

He took another bite of his shrimp. "Did she really like to take wrong turns, or did she have a bad sense of direction too?"

She giggled as he'd hoped she would. "No, I get that from my dad. Mom and Auntie were always the navigators. She just liked to see new things. I took over her shop for her every summer in college while she traveled. I don't think she ever made it to Hawaii, but she would have loved it." She mock-leered at him. "Auntie probably would have pinched your butt and called you a stud muffin."

"And you plan to do that when you reach old age?"

Her eyes twinkled merrily, but her shrug was demure. "Sure. I'll need something to keep me entertained. Harassing hot men who can't get mad at an old lady sounds like fun."

For some reason, he could picture her being a holy terror as a senior citizen, a wicked gleam in her gaze as she shook up people's lives the way she had his. He could imagine how amusing it would be to sit back as an old man and watch the show. Maybe she wouldn't grab anyone's ass, but she'd still be finding ways to have a good time no matter where she happened to be. She'd probably manage to drag other people into that fun. Now there was a way to spend his retirement. He shook his head at those ridiculous thoughts. It would be too good to be true. Hell, *Julie* seemed too good to be true.

It was a futile idea, but he suddenly wondered how much different his life would have been—how much different *he* would have been—if he'd met Julie before Lilith. Would he be the bitter divorcee who was suspicious of every woman's motives? Would he still be blown away by the force of nature that was Hurricane Julie?

He didn't know, and it was foolish to wonder. He was who he was. He'd made the choices he'd made, and his life had been shaped because of those choices.

"They have a portable sink set up over there." Julie pointed before she stood and gathered her plate and fork. She waggled her eyebrows at him. "I bet they even have soap."

"Wow, do you really think so? I'm positively giddy with excitement," he returned, *sotto voce*.

She rolled her eyes. "Come on. We need to get back on the road, and then I need to explain a flat tire to the rental company."

"They might be assholes about that."

"I know, but that's a problem for later. I'm not letting it get me down now." She waved that away. "But, Lukas?"

He paused in collecting a napkin that had been caught in the sea breeze. "Yes?"

Her gaze was direct. "Thanks for listening, about my aunt and mom. Thanks for not judging. Thanks for asking in the first place."

And he almost hadn't bothered to ask, hadn't wanted to get involved, hadn't wanted to intrude. He'd always been a bit reserved with new people—Julie being a notable exception—but how much more withdrawn had he become in recent years? He was glad he'd ignored his usual reticence for her. She was a nice woman, and if his listening had helped with what she was going through, he was even gladder. When she left the island, he hoped she was in a better place with her grief than she had been when she arrived.

"You're welcome." He walked around the table and dropped a kiss on her forehead. "Let's get going."

"Turn in here," Lukas said and Julie obeyed without question. He hadn't steered her wrong so far, so she assumed he knew where he was going.

After cutting across the highway, she pulled into a small parking lot surrounded by trees. Between the trunks, she could see glimpses of sand and ocean. "Where are we?"

"Other than the North Shore? I'm not sure. It just looked like a pretty place to stop." He winked. "I thought Aunt Eloise would have approved of the spontaneity."

"Ha. Yes, she would have." Julie set the parking brake and climbed out of the car. They walked through the trees, which dappled the ground with shadow. Pretty, just as Lukas promised, but nothing could beat the moment they broke through to the beach.

The breeze curled around her, the scent of the ocean filling her nose. The waves crashing against the shore were so blue and beautiful it was almost surreal. The beach was dotted with palm trees, the sandy coastline stretching between two black cliffs. And she'd thought Waikiki Beach was gorgeous. It had nothing on this.

Lukas's arm came around her shoulder. Neither of them said anything, just stood there and enjoyed the stunning panorama.

"Let's walk a little," he suggested. He kept his hold on her, and their shoulders and hips bumped as they walked, but it felt like the most normal thing in the world. Being with him was comfortable, but he also sparked a fire inside her that she'd never experienced with any other man before. It confused her, because the first reaction was one she associated with a friend, the second with a lover. None of her boyfriends had ever hit both notes for her at once. They'd always been too much of one or the other, and it hadn't worked out.

When they reached the towering black cliff, Lukas steered them into an alcove in the rock face. She looked up at the jagged outcrop-pings of stone. "Is it lava rock?"

"I'm not sure, but it seems like a good guess." His voice sounded in her ear, his hot breath brushing over her neck. He pressed a kiss to her nape, then nipped at the tender flesh there. Her eyes closed and her head dropped back on his shoulder.

Goose bumps broke across her skin as he drew her against him. He was big and solid and warm behind her. Passion shimmered within her, and she savored the burn. They were half an island away from their hotel and she had a feeling the rest of the drive was going to be a little bit torturous with them trapped together in that teeny little car, close but not close enough. His palms skimmed down her sides until he reached her skirt, then gathered fistfuls of the fabric. Her eyes popped open in shock and the hard length of his erection pushed against her backside. "You have to be kidding me, Lukas."

His voice was low and rough, cajoling. "We're shielded from the road here."

Pulling away, she spun to face him, hands planted on hips. "Anyone could come along and see us! Aren't all beaches in Hawaii public?"

"Yes, so we'd better hurry before we get caught." His smile was challenging, and she couldn't believe the restrained professor wanted to do the nasty in public. He caught her hand and drew her further into the alcove, sitting on the sand with his back to the cliff. He tugged her down until she was straddling his lap. The sand was rough under her knees, but she didn't try to get up. Excitement spurted through her, even though she wasn't sure this was the best idea ever.

He smoothed his hands up her thighs. "I'm so glad you're wearing a dress, even if it sucked to change a flat tire in it."

A shiver rippled over her skin, her breath rushing faster. He pulled her forward until her sex pressed against his. He was hard, straining against his fly. Lust punched through her, and she felt her core grow damp with need. She set her hands on his shoulders to steady herself. The pounding of her pulse filled her ears, competing with the crash of waves on the shore.

"Kiss me, *mein Liebling*." He traced the edge of her panties around the bottom of her buttocks, and her inner muscles clenched.

There was no refusing him, no denying the heat and fire he created inside her. Leaning in, she offered him her mouth, and he took it, took her, and she moaned. Their tongues twined, the flavor of him reached down deep and grabbed something inside her she couldn't even identify, but it felt amazing.

She was really going to do this. The thrill of danger and the forbidden raced through her, sizzling her nerve endings. Pressing her hips forward to grind her herself against his hard length increased the ache of longing within her. She could feel the beginnings of climax shivering through her. A groan vibrated his broad chest. He thrust his tongue into her mouth, the motion mimicking what she wanted him to be doing to other parts of her anatomy. Unstoppable desire built like a rising tide inside her, and she had to have him moving deep in her sex, driving her toward orgasm. *Yes. Oh God, yes.*

By pushing her hand between them, she could fumble with his belt and zipper. When she got his pants open, she reached in to free him and fondled his thick erection. Moisture beaded at the tip and she smeared it over the bulbous crest. He shuddered, his hips bucking beneath her.

"Condom," he gasped after he tore his mouth from hers.

He set her away from him just long enough to pull a rubber out of his wallet. She grabbed it out of his hands, ripped it open, and slid it on his hard length. Her body throbbed, so close to the edge she thought she might explode into a million pieces.

"Impatient, much?" His chuckle was a rough sound.

She shot him a look. "If you're not inside me in the next thirty seconds, I'm going to come without you."

"*Mein Gott*, Julie!" He didn't even bother to remove her panties, just jerked the inset aside and thrust into her. The stretch was exquisite and when he began nudging back and forth within her, the friction was intense enough to make her eyes roll back.

"Lukas!" she gasped. "This is insane."

"I know." His arms encircled her and pulled her even closer while he worked his full length into her sex. "You feel so perfect, all tight and wet around me."

His words sent an electric shock straight to her core, and she had to move, to push toward the climax that teased her senses. She arched into him, lifting and lowering herself on his length. She rode him faster and faster, her breath rushing out in gasps. The muscles in her thighs burned as she quickened her pace, and her knees in the sand were more than a little uncomfortable, but she couldn't have stopped for anything.

Rocking his pelvis upwards, he increased the depth and speed of his penetration. His hands closed over her breasts, massaging before he zeroed in on her nipples. He pinched them hard through her dress, twisting until she cried out with pleasured pain. It sent her tumbling straight into orgasm. Tingles raced over her skin, and her inner muscles fisted in rhythmic pulses on his pounding shaft. She ground herself down on the coarse hair at his groin, extending her climax as long as possible.

His fingers bit into hips, so tight it was almost bruising. He pulled her to the base of his erection, forcing himself deeper inside her than he'd been before. The shock sent her over the edge again, and her inner muscles squeezed around his shaft. His groan was a harsh, wonderful sound. He shuddered beneath her, his gaze locking with hers and she watched satisfaction play across his face.

"Julie," he whispered.

Just her name, but he looked at her like she was the most amazing thing to ever rock his world. She liked being looked at that way. It made her feel powerful, irresistible, sexy.

A girl could get used to feeling that way.

CHAPTER
seven

L ukas stared blindly out the car window as they cruised toward Honolulu. Thankfully, Julie just needed to stay on the highway because he didn't think he was up to any serious navigating.

She was right, what they'd done *had* been insane. Irresponsible. Irresistible. What was it about her that made him set his caution aside? Hell, he'd thrown it to the wind. A cautious man doesn't have sex on a public beach in broad daylight. Yet, he'd done exactly that, because waiting another two hours to have her was more than he could stand. It had been mind-blowing, earth-shattering. It was getting better every time, and if anyone had asked him if that was possible the first night they'd spent together, he would have said no.

Her hand touched his shoulder. "Hey, you okay? Did I wear you out?"

"Hardly." He tossed her a quick grin. "Though it was a little out of character for me."

"Me too, but it sure was fun." She bit her lip. "Wanna do it again?

In bed, this time. Or in a room that locks."

He could picture many different ways to have her in his hotel room. On the desk, against the wall, in the shower. Not to mention the variety of positions that were possible in his king-size bed. His body reacted predictably to that line of thinking and he shifted in his seat. "Yes."

"So cooperative." She hummed her approval. "What do you do for fun when you're not in Hawaii?"

He blinked at the sudden change of topic, but considering the constriction in his shorts, he was grateful for it. Getting his mind off getting in her pants was a good idea. At least until they reached the hotel.

Before he got his brain in gear enough to respond, she answered her own question, "I read a lot. Actually, I listen to a lot of audio books while I'm knitting or crocheting. I also like old movies. Hanging out on the beach, obviously, since I live in a town right on the coast."

"Have you been to the Stanford Theatre in Palo Alto?" When she shook her head, he continued, "It's a restored Art Deco theater from the silent movie era, so there's an organ that comes up out of the stage. They play music during the intermission between movies. One ticket and you're in for two movies, plus the popcorn is the most delicious thing you've ever tasted. It's addictive."

"Crack-sprinkled goodness, huh?" Interest laced the amusement in her voice.

He chuckled. "Yeah, something like that. I can't believe you've never been there."

"I'll have to check it out some time," she remarked, her tone casual.

She didn't mention going with him while she did so, but it quivered on the tip of his tongue to ask her. He could try to deny it, but he wanted to share one of his favorite activities with her. He loved coming to Hawaii, and he'd loved sharing it with her the last few days. Would the Stanford Theatre be any different? He somehow doubted it. Her endless zest for life would make anything entertaining.

She flicked on her blinker to switch lanes and passed a slow-moving car. "What about you, Professor? What do you do for fun?"

"Other than catching a showing at the Stanford Theatre?" He creased his shorts between his fingers. "I like to swim and I rent a catamaran occasionally for some sailing in the bay. I spend a lot of time on my research, writing articles for publication, advising students. It's not just teaching classes, you know?"

She nodded. "Yeah, running a business takes a lot of time too. I get having a job that consumes much of your life."

"Academia does that." Something several women he'd dated in the past had complained about, especially when he'd been struggling to establish himself in the field and maneuvering through campus politics to get tenure. His work had had to take precedence over a lot of other things, which hadn't exactly pleased the women in his life. He swallowed and decided that wasn't something he wanted to discuss. Topic change. "Have you ever been sailing on a catamaran?"

She stirred in her seat, glancing at him quickly. "Not on a catamaran, no, but I do like sailing. My mother made me take lessons with her when I was in high school, and it was one of the things we enjoyed together. I haven't been out on the water in years though."

Could she be any more perfect? The woman knew how to sail. It was like some strange deity had fashioned a woman that would appeal to him the most and then tossed her into his life. Just to tempt him with what he could never have. "They do sailing trips here, so maybe we should go. There are snorkeling trips and sunset cruises."

She sighed, and he thought there was a hint of disappointment in the sound, but when he looked at her, she was smiling. "Let's check the prices and see how steep it is."

"The concierge would know all that, so we can ask when we get back."

It would give them a good reason to spend more time together. Julie didn't seem to need a reason, but Lukas liked having the excuse anyway. It made it easier to justify his sudden craving to have someone around all the time. He was an introvert by nature, and enjoyed time he had to himself, which was what he'd thought he'd be doing after his conference. An opportunity to recharge from the constant barrage of scholars in his field, but he didn't have any trouble being with Julie.

He still wasn't sure if that was a good thing or a bad thing, but he suspected the latter.

A fter a shower, Julie hustled to change into jeans and a T-shirt. Lukas was meeting her downstairs in a few minutes, and they were going to check out a nearby café called the Wailana Coffee House. She'd taken more time in the bathroom than she should have, but after changing a tire and doing the deed on a beach, she'd needed to scrub every crevice of her body. It was amazing the places sand could find its way into. There'd even been grains buried in her bra. She knew that part of her anatomy had come nowhere near the ground, but it had turned into a sandbox anyway. Gross, but that was what showers were for.

Yanking a brush through her wind-tangled hair, she winced when she hit a snarl. She winced again when her phone rang and Anne's ring tone blared out. She'd managed to avoid her friends' messages the day before, but that couldn't go on forever without them getting worried. She went into the bedroom and picked up the cell to answer it. "Hey,

Anne."

"Sorry, it's Meg on Anne's phone." Meg's voice was filled with undisguised glee. "She lost a bet with Finn and has to give his tomcat a bath. I decided to use the opportunity to steal her phone and call you. I figured you'd be too scared not to pick up a call from Anne."

"Jesus, I'm not that scary!" The echoing sound of Anne's voice came from the background. She must be in the bathroom scrubbing the cat now. Julie had met that tom before and she wouldn't get within ten feet of him. He was one mean kitty.

"And yet, she picked up your call," Meg retorted.

The only response was a decidedly feline yowl, and Julie bit back a horrified laugh. Poor Anne. That must have been one hell of a bet to lose.

Meg snickered. "So...inquiring minds want to know who occupied the man-sized shoes beside you in the picture. Your feet looked rather chummy."

"She found a cabana boy," Anne shouted from the background.

Sighing, Julie gave in. She wasn't sure she was ready to share everything she'd been feeling and doing with Lukas—perhaps because she hadn't sorted it all out for herself yet—but her friends were smart enough to know when she was hiding something and persistent enough to pry it out of her. "He's not a cabana boy. He's a physics professor."

"Oh, nice." Meg hummed. "Smart is sexy."

"Who's smart?" Anne asked. "At least put the phone on speaker so I can hear too."

"Hang on," Meg said. There was a soft beep and then the connection became a little more static-filled. "Julie said the guy was a physics professor and I said that smart is sexy. There, you're all caught up, Anne."

A hiss and snarl came through the line, then Anne asked, "The really important question isn't what he does for a living, it's did you bang him yet?"

"Yes, I did."

She whooped gleefully. "Go, Julie! I knew you could do it."

"We really need to muzzle her," Julie said, rolling her eyes even though her friends couldn't see it.

Meg snorted. "Tell me about it. We can get a matching one for the drama llama mama."

"She's being extra bad this year?" Though how much *extra* Anne's mom could possibly get in the bad department, Julie wasn't sure. The woman was a world champ of drama. Julie picked up her brush and went to work on her hair again. She still had to finish getting ready for dinner.

Meg groaned. "I have never been so grateful to get an impromptu visit from anyone when Finn's dad and his girlfriend showed up at his house. They were planning a skiing trip, but there's a snowstorm in Banff, so they switched their tickets to SFO."

"Thank God for bad weather, then." Julie got the last tangle out of her hair and then went to dig through her suitcase for a bra and panties.

"Uh. Huh." Meg's voice dropped. "Karen's not been so lucky. She and Tate had a huge fight. She's camping out on Anne's couch. I think...they might be breaking up."

Julie's knees went weak and she stumbled back to plop on the side of the bed. Her stomach tightened. "Oh no."

"Are you really surprised?" Meg asked quietly.

"No, but I'm really sad for her."

She sighed. "Hugo seems positively cheerful compared to her."

Since Meg's depressive basset hound always seemed borderline suicidal, that was really saying something. Julie shook her head. "Ouch."

Anne answered, and her voice was clearer, as if she was closer to the phone. "If that idiot could have taken a few minutes away from his work to pay attention to Karen, this wouldn't have happened. It's too bad. I always liked Tate, even if he was an all-work no-play workaholic."

"Me too," Julie and Meg said.

Julie remembered being a bridesmaid at the wedding, and Karen had looked so damn happy. It was hard to remember exactly when that happiness had faded and the discontent had begun to reflect on her friend's face whenever she talked about her husband. Poor Karen. All that promise and love and it had gone up in smoke. Julie had had her fair share of breakups, and they were never easy, but a divorce had to be so much worse.

Her chest squeezed tight in sympathy. "Is there anything I can do from here? Would a phone call help, or would she rather not talk about it right now?"

"I think she asked to stay on my couch instead of Meg's because she knew my family would be a distraction...and because Finn and Meg being all love birdy would have made her feel worse." For once, the indomitable Anne was subdued. "She hasn't wanted to talk about it at all, so if you do call her, make sure you discuss anything else, okay?"

"Okay." Julie let out a slow breath. "You'll give her a hug from me?"

"I will," Meg promised.

"Do you guys know what the fight was about?" Splitting up during the holidays had to be hard. That must have been one nasty blowup, especially since Karen was usually pretty even-keeled. Which had always been a nice balance in their group. Meg and Karen were the ones who found a way out of trouble when Anne decided to try something crazy and Julie had egged her on because she wanted to know if it would be any fun.

Fun. The word hadn't been part of Julie's vocabulary for the last year, but as she'd told Lukas, she was doing better. She'd bet if she talked to him about what was going on with Karen, he'd understand. He'd been through a divorce, and he might have some ideas for how to help her friend get through this. It was amazing how easy Julie found it to confide in him. She'd told him things she'd never even told her best friends.

Meg broke into her thoughts. "We haven't heard what they fought over, no. Karen hasn't said and we've been too afraid to push. She's looking pretty fragile right now, so we're just trying to keep her occupied with holiday preparations. Anne's nutty sisters have actually been a big help on that score. You know they need a full-time referee when they get together."

"Yeah, and that's usually my job, but I'm letting Karen handle them this time," Anne said. "It's been entertaining to watch. They've never seen her lay down the law before. My mom was doing her drama queen routine, and she was so shocked she about crapped her pants when Karen told her to suck it up and grow a pair."

"Ha." Julie giggled. "I've been telling people for years that she's tougher than she looks."

Meg huffed. "She had to be to deal with the two of you over the years. We'd both have been gray-haired and locked in a loony bin before we graduated high school if we *hadn't* grown a pair."

Julie dissolved into laughter, while Anne protested, "Ah, come on. We weren't *that* bad. We never got you guys arrested or anything."

"Well," countered Julie, "there was that one time Auntie Eloise had to talk the cops out of impounding my car because we were speeding down Highway 1 so fast."

"Only because we were trying to get away from that motorcycle gang who didn't take it so well when I hosed them down with grape juice." Anne's voice rose. "It was an accident, I swear!"

That did it. Gales of laughter followed Anne's claims of innocence, and Julie had to wipe tears from her eyes. "We had some good times, didn't we?"

"You called that a *good* time?" Meg queried. "Karen and I were shitting bricks in the backseat."

"No, what made it a good time was telling Auntie Eloise what happened and watching her try to be stern and not laugh."

Meg chortled. "Okay, yeah, that was funny. You're just lucky your parents were out of town that weekend and that Eloise didn't snitch on you."

"She didn't have to. The cops did, remember?" Julie had been grounded for two months for that one. It probably would have been worse, but her parents had been shocked that she'd gotten into serious mischief like that. Normally, their high jinks had been a little less illegal.

"Yeah, but if your parents had been there, your car would have been impounded," Meg argued. "Which is worse than being grounded."

"True," Julie conceded.

"All's well that ends well," Anne said cheerfully. "And, Jules?"

"Yeah?"

"You sound better than you have in a while. I think getting laid agrees with you."

"Me too. A hot island romance is just what I needed for the holidays." Julie didn't mention that Lukas lived close by, so her friends would have no idea how plausible seeing him after they left the island would be. She didn't want to admit how appealing that option was.

She'd laughed more in the last couple of days than she had in the past couple of months combined. She felt like she was rediscovering parts of herself that had been dormant for the last year. Maybe she wasn't as vivacious and audacious as Eloise had been, but she knew how to have a good time. Not that she wanted to be as big an instigator as she had been in high school, but she'd been a pretty happy person before the depression of losing her great-aunt had engulfed her life. She could get back to that. She *needed* to get back to it.

"All right, ladies. I have a dinner date with a certain professor. Take care and tell Karen I'll call her later. Give her my love."

"We will," Meg replied. "Have a good time, sweetie."

Anne was blunter. "Get your groove on for all of us. With Meg's future in-laws in town, even she's not getting any play right now. It's a sad sexless bunch back home."

What did you say to something like that? Anne had a way of leaving everyone speechless. Julie rolled her eyes. "Well, I guess I'll have to take one for the team, huh? Night, guys!"

Meg and Anne were still giggling when Julie hung up on them. Time to go meet Lukas and take one for the team. It was a tough job, but somebody had to do it.

CHAPTER EIGHT

C hristmas Day was pure bliss. They did nothing but stay in bed together, watch TV, make love, and order room service when they got hungry. Sure, it didn't have all the trappings of the holidays—there was no tree, no presents, but the day was perfect anyway. Lukas let contentment unfurl inside of him.

They lay sprawled across the sheets, still naked from the last round of mattress gymnastics. Her head rested on his shoulder and he was flipping through channels. "How about *It's a Wonderful Life?* It is a Christmas classic."

She nodded, and her hair slid against his skin. "True, and it ends just in time to get ready for dinner."

"Do we have plans to do anything other than stay right here?" He stroked a lazy hand up and down her side.

"Yes, we do." She sat up and pressed a palm to his chest.

"Oh?" He lifted one eyebrow. "Care to let me in on the plans?"

"Well, *I* have plans anyway." She offered up a gamine grin. "Since you let me horn in on your reservation the other night, would you like to do the same with me? I'm having Christmas dinner at the Royal Hawaiian—I'd love to have you join me."

He hummed quietly. "And I would love to join you."

It sounded as good as anything else, and it meant he'd be with her. He couldn't think of anything he'd enjoy more.

"Good, then." She scooted to the edge of the bed and grabbed her cell phone. "Let me just change my reservation. They might be pickier about it that the Rainbow Lanai was."

He watched her make the call, which he'd done several times today as she'd rung her father, her shop assistant, and each one of her friends. She'd been cheerful and upbeat after all of those calls, except one.

When she hung up, she bounced on the mattress. "Reservation changed."

"I forgot to ask how your friend is doing today. Karen, isn't it?"

It was getting easier to ask those kinds of questions—personal, prying questions. It was getting easier to answer them when she asked, too. He'd stopped beating himself up over it. The woman had gotten under his defenses. Hell, he wasn't even sure he'd had any defenses when it came to her. She'd disarmed him the moment he'd seen her laughing at the rain, before she'd ever said a word to him.

His only saving grace was this would be over in two more days. He ignored the stab of pain in his chest at the thought.

"Yeah, her name is Karen." Her face softened. "She's keeping busy. My friends are with her, and I'll be back in a couple of days to lend a hand." She pushed her rumpled hair back from her forehead. "It's funny, I thought I was going to have the shittiest Christmas, being without Eloise, but Karen easily has me beat. Isn't that sad?"

"Yes, it is." He held out his hand, and she crawled over until she could settle against him. "It'll get easier for her, just as it will for you.

It's just a different kind of loss."

Simple words, but he still hadn't managed to overcome all of his hang-ups from his divorce. He knew his circumstances with Lilith were extreme, but he could only hope the recovery was smoother for Julie's friend. A breakup was difficult even under the best of circumstances.

"How long did it take to get easier for you?"

There was a question that cut right to the quick. He fought a wince. "With my father, it took a year or two before it stopped hurting so bad every time I thought about him. I still miss him though."

"I meant—"

"My divorce, I know." He heaved a sigh, sliding his palm up and down her bare back. The last thing he wanted to talk about when he was in bed with Julie was the downfall of his marriage. But if it helped to ease her worry for her friend, then he couldn't deny her. Maybe that made him an idiot, but there it was. Even then, he couldn't tell her the whole truth. Very few people knew what had happened with Lilith, how bad it had truly gotten, and he didn't want Julie to know. That was a stroll down memory lane he never wanted to take again. "I'm sure her breakup won't be as bad as mine. Our divorce strung out for almost two years before it was settled."

"Wow, that's crazy."

He rolled a shoulder in the most casual shrug he could manage. It felt more like a spasmodic jerk. "Told you it was the divorce from hell."

"I don't think it'll be like that for Karen and Tate. If he wanted to hold on to the marriage, he would have tried a little harder while he was in it." She didn't seem to notice when Lukas tensed. Her words scraped across old wounds. Some men didn't try, but Lukas hadn't been one of them. He'd worked like hell to save his marriage and it hadn't meant a damn thing in the end. It just made him an even bigger fool for trying so hard. Julie frowned, her fingers curling into his chest hair. "I'm betting Tate doesn't put up a fight at all, which is sad too. Karen's worth fighting for. All my friends are. They're awesome."

"You're lucky to have each other." His voice came out rougher than he meant it to.

Her head came up and she searched his face, but just said, "I know. They had my back when my mom died. And Eloise. I couldn't have made it through the last twelve months without them." She lifted a hand and stroked her fingertip down his cheekbone. "What about you? Who helped you get through your divorce? You talk about your colleagues, but not your friends. I'm starting to think you don't have any."

Another sore point. "Mmm, yeah, that's a more complicated question than you think. I met my ex not long after I came to America, so most of the friends we made were...couple friends."

Her expression was sympathetic, her palm curving over his jaw. "And she got custody in the divorce?"

"Something like that." The reality was, he hadn't known how to talk to anyone about what he was dealing with. It was insane and sometimes he'd thought it was making *him* insane too. Not a chat to have with the husband of his wife's best friend. "I threw myself into my career after that. It was simpler, so those friends and I just drifted apart."

She nodded. "What about before you came stateside? No old German cronies?"

That made one corner of his mouth tilt up. Better memories there. "I have a few friends from when I was growing up. We keep in touch over email, but being so far apart means that life gets in the way a lot. Though we try to get together whenever I go back to visit my mother."

"What are their names?" She tapped the tip of his nose.

"Dieter."

Her brows arched expectantly. "And...that's it? I only get one name?"

He widened his eyes innocently. "That's all I have to give you. There were three of them, all named Dieter."

She propped herself up on his chest and stared down at him. "Your three best friends had the *same name?* How did you distinguish between them when you were talking? 'Hey, Dieter' wouldn't be that helpful."

"We usually just called each other by last name. It worked for us." Reaching up, he swept a hand through her hair, just for the pleasure of touching her.

"What are the Dieters' last names?"

"Schmidt, Hoffmann, and Meyer."

"Schmidt, Hoffmann, Meyer, and Klein." She rolled the words out slowly. "It sounds like a law firm."

That made him chuckle. "One of them became a lawyer. One owns a landscaping business, and the other is gainfully unemployed with a very wealthy wife."

She made a little noise in her throat. "A German sugar mama, huh? Impressive."

He tsked and shook his head. "Sorry. She's Swiss."

"Ah, of course. I should have guessed." She threw up a hand. "I mean, that's not special at all. Doesn't *everyone* have a Swiss sugar mama?"

"Absolutely everyone." He pressed his lips together. "I have two."

She buried her face against his chest, her shoulders quaking with laughter. "Oh my God."

Being reminded of better times, of who he'd been before his life imploded, was both a blessing and a curse. He wasn't that man anymore, didn't have that idealistic streak any longer. Perhaps that was why he'd let so many of his friendships go. Not just because he didn't know how to tell them what he was going through, but because he didn't want to think about the younger, more innocent him that his friends had once known. He'd have to see the bitter disappointment he'd become reflected back in their eyes. Maybe it was easier to have people in his life who hadn't known him before. People like Julie, who accepted who he was now, and didn't expect him to be someone different.

Maybe he just needed to get a life. He fought a self-derisive snort and rolled his eyes at himself. *Suck it up, Klein. It's Christmas. Save the depressing shit for New Year's.*

Folding one arm behind his head, he waited until she looked at him again before he spoke. "I thought we were supposed to be watching *It's a Wonderful Life.*"

She leaned up and kissed him. Their lips clung together, and she slipped her tongue in to tangle with his. "Mmm, forget the movie. You can rent it. I have a better idea about what we can do until dinner."

"Oh, really?" He pressed the mute button and tossed the remote aside. "Tell me all about it."

The Royal Hawaiian Hotel was pink. Very, very pink. In-your-face *pink*. To emphasize what no one could possibly miss, they had pink Christmas trees scattered throughout the lobby.

"Well, it makes a statement," Lukas commented. His voice was carefully neutral, which told Julie he was probably trying not to snicker.

She arched her eyebrows as she looked around. "I wouldn't go for this at home, but I think it's pretty. If you're going to do pink, do it big."

"Go big or go home?" He slid his hands in his pockets, eyeing the various shades of rose and fuchsia and mauve and magenta as if they might jump out and bite him.

She bit her lip and shook her finger at him. "Exactly."

"You look beautiful tonight, by the way." His grin was boyish. "You look beautiful every night, but especially now."

"Thank you." She did a little twirl for him. Her wrap was a pale blue silk, her darker navy dress was fitted and sparkled just a little, and the heels she'd purchased the day she'd arrived went with the outfit even better than the ones she'd forgotten at home.

After pulling a hand free, he skimmed the fringe of her wrap. "You made this as well, right?"

"Right." She drew the shawl up, knowing that its color complemented her skin. She'd fallen in love with the yarn and just had to have it, and the airy lace pattern she'd used turned out better than she'd expected.

He bent down to kiss the side of her neck. "It's lovely. And you look lovely wearing it."

A shiver raced down her skin, and her body warmed, even though they'd gone at it so often today that she should be incapable of response. He just got to her. Turning her head to catch his lips, she kissed him. "*Danke.*"

"*Bitte.*" His hands settled on her hips, not drawing her closer, but making the embrace more intimate. Something about this entire day had felt more intimate, as if she'd seen more of the real Lukas. Not that he'd held back in the days they'd been together—she couldn't put her finger on what was different, but she liked it.

He nibbled on her lower lip, his blue eyes meeting hers as they pulled apart.

"Ready for dinner?" He offered her an arm, and she looped hers through it.

"Absolutely. We have a few minutes to check out the sea view. There's a sitting area at the end of the hall that's supposed to overlook the Pacific." She led the way and grinned when she reached the massive room. There were white arches, wood ceilings, polished floors and miles of plush throw rugs. Beyond the arches were manicured lawns and then the ocean. The atmosphere of the place was decadent and lush.

She cast a glance at Lukas. "Oooh, fancy."

"That's what they want you to think." He chuckled.

"Then they're wildly successful." She tugged on his arm to steer him toward the restaurant. "Let's see if the food is as good as the ambiance."

In under ten minutes, they were seated and the waitress had brought them each a glass of wine. The restaurant was every bit as beautifully appointed as the lobby and sitting room, and she let herself goggle just a bit at the sumptuous décor. She was used to much simpler settings for her meals, but she liked being able to do something special to celebrate the holiday.

She toasted him. "Merry Christmas, Lukas."

"*Frohe Weihnachten*, Julie." He clinked his glass against hers, the look in his gaze warm enough to make her heart squeeze. She wouldn't mind having a man look at her like that every day for the rest of her life.

"This vacation has turned out far better than I expected. I just wanted to have a nice getaway. Instead, I got someone to share it with." She sipped her wine, and its smooth taste lingered on her tongue.

His smile was endearingly self-effacing. "Glad I could improve the situation."

"You really did." She set her glass down and toyed with the delicate stem. "Thank you for listening to all of my problems the last few days, especially about Karen. You've been really helpful."

"I'm sorry about her marriage." He swirled his wine around, his gaze on the deep red liquid. "What about you? We've talked about my past. What about yours? Have you ever been in a serious relationship?"

She tilted her head at the change in topic but saw no reason not to answer. She'd certainly pried into his past, so turnabout was fair play. "Several. One just out of college, but we were too young. A couple since then. One even proposed, but it was his way of trying to salvage a relationship that was already floundering."

"Fish or cut bait?" He lifted a single brow, which said very clearly what he thought of that kind of attitude.

She twisted her lips. "I think that's how he was feeling."

"Why was it floundering?"

Making a face, she sat back in her chair. "He kind of wanted a stay-at-home mom type, like when we married and had kids, I knew he'd want me to give up everything to raise kids and have a hot meal on the table when he got home from work."

"Not what you want?" His gaze was probing enough that she squirmed a bit. This shouldn't be an uncomfortable topic. She knew what she wanted, but she'd never found it. Until now. That was the awkward part. Lukas had all the qualities she wanted in a man, only she couldn't keep him.

She licked her lower lip. "I wouldn't mind a kid or two, and I don't judge women who choose the stay-at-home mom gig, but it's not for me. I feel like I'd resent my children if I were locked in the house with them all day and had nothing that was just for myself."

The waitress broke in to their conversation when she walked up to set a bread basket on their table. "Hi, folks. Have you had a chance to look over the menu? Can I answer any questions?"

"No questions from me. I'm ready to order." He glanced at Julie. "Are you?"

"Everything looks good." An all-day sexfest could certainly work up an appetite.

"Everything *is* good. The chef let me taste test it all." The waitress grinned conspiratorially. She was probably in her fifties, with a few crow's feet around her eyes and a friendly demeanor. "So, where are you fine folks from?"

Julie cradled her wine glass between her palms. "I'm from California, a little south of San Francisco."

"Nice! Welcome to Hawaii." Their server glanced at Lukas. "And you?"

"Also from California." He offered no more information than that, deflecting personal questions the way he usually did with strangers. He was never unfriendly, but he rarely chatted or teased with anyone they'd met. Except with Julie. She got to see a funnier, sweeter side of him than he showed the rest of the world. She had no idea what she'd done to get him to open up even that much, but she was glad for it.

"Ladies first." Lukas gestured to Julie to allow her to order.

She took another swig of her wine. "I'll have the prawns, please."

The waitress nodded and jotted down the order on her notepad. "And for you, sir?"

"The prime rib."

When the other woman walked away, his bearing became more relaxed and he gave Julie an easy smile. He was clearly an introvert, but she also thought part of his behavior might cover up the fact that he was a little shy. Remaining quiet was a coping mechanism he must have learned over the years, but it pleased her that he seemed so comfortable around her.

"Back to our conversation." He tilted the bread basket toward her, giving her first choice. "What you said makes sense to me. My career is very important to me."

She snagged a roll, broke it open, and slathered a bit of butter on it. "Well, it wasn't so much my career. I was managing an office until Aunt Eloise got sick, and I walked away from that to come help her, but...I was still doing something I loved. It's hard to put a fine point on the distinction, but if I'd had to be Eloise's live-in caretaker, I might have gone nuts. Working in Purl Moon was different."

He waved his butter knife through the air. "I understand the distinction."

"Do you?" She bit into her roll.

"Absolutely." He shrugged as if it were the most obvious thing in the world. "I wouldn't want to be a stay-at-home dad or live-in caretaker. It's a demanding, all-consuming role that makes you sacrifice some of your sense of self."

"*Yes.* Exactly." She spread her hands. "So, I guess my kids will have to deal with a nanny or daycare. It'll give them something to tell their therapist about when they grow up."

"Don't be so sure." He huffed out a breath. "Some of my students have those helicopter parents, who want to call me and check on their grades or come in with them for academic advising. Terrifying people. Not only have they sacrificed their sense of self, they've subsumed some of their child's identity and independence too."

She choked on a giggle, even though it was more horrifying than funny. That was exactly the kind of person she didn't want to become, and that her almost-fiancé wanted to turn her into. "So together, they're one person?"

"Probably more truthful than anyone would like to admit," he replied drily. "As you said, we all have to make choices on how to live our lives, raise children, navigate careers. I need things in my life that are just for me, even if that is a bit selfish."

"I kind of love you right now." The words escaped before she gave them any thought, and it shocked her how much truth there might be in them. She covered it with a quick, disarming smile. "That was something I couldn't get the last guy to understand no matter how much we talked about it. I'm glad I'm not the only one who thinks that way."

"We birds of a feather must flock together." He didn't skip a beat when he spoke, so she had to assume he took her profession of love as a joke. Which was how she'd meant it. Mostly.

It quivered on the tip of her tongue to ask if he'd be willing to see her when they got back to California. She barely managed to bite back the words. Despite the deepening feeling of closeness, she still wasn't sure how receptive he'd be to something like that. If all he wanted was a vacation affair, and she asked for more now, she had a feeling he'd withdraw faster than she could blink.

There were secrets and shadows that lurked in his eyes, and he always seemed to be holding back a little. She wanted to know why, but for that, she'd need more time. She wanted that time. The longer they'd been together, the more certain she'd been that he was exactly the kind of guy she'd want to get to know better. And it wasn't the kind of knowing that had anything to do with sex. It was the deeper intimacy of sharing lives and experiences. She wanted to try that with him.

Unlike many of the other men she'd dated, Lukas didn't seem to want her to be anything other than herself: funny, sometimes goofy, and just serious enough not to qualify as perky. They seemed to agree on a lot of things, some mundane and some important. The potential between them was so ripe she could taste it, but she was too scared to lose this fragile *thing* they had.

Maybe she'd muster up the courage to ask the day before they left. That way, if he wasn't interested in more, she wouldn't lose out on any of the time she could have spent with him.

Yes, it was chickening out, but only a little.

CHAPTER NINE

L ukas woke up with a soft, warm woman draped across his chest. Julie. He smiled before he even opened his eyes. She felt good there—right. Maybe it was an incredibly stupid thought to have, but he didn't take it back.

I kind of love you right now.

Her words the night before had been in jest, but he let himself imagine how it would feel if it were true. What would it be like to be loved by a woman like Julie?

Heaven.

Or hell, if it all went wrong.

Didn't everything go wrong, eventually? But he clicked with Julie so well, it was like nothing he'd ever experienced before. It gave him something fragile and terrifying, something he didn't even know he was still capable of.

Hope.

It was an awful, wretched thing, hope. It set a person up for a huge fall. Yet he couldn't help thinking...what if? What if he gave this thing a shot? What if he tried, just one last time? He squeezed his eyes shut, sighing. The fact that he was even thinking along these lines went a long way toward violating his no-relationship policy. He'd fought against the pull she had on him, but it seemed to be a losing battle.

They were flying home tomorrow, and the idea of never seeing her again was a knife to the chest. He didn't want to give her up. Not yet. It wasn't the first time he'd had this thought in the last week. The risk seemed huge, like a deep, dark chasm opening under his feet and he didn't know where the bottom was or if he could find the necessary courage to step over the edge. Because he knew already that he couldn't have something casual with Julie. He felt too much for her as it was. With Julie, it would be serious, and far more real than anything he'd allowed himself in...years.

Clammy sweat slicked his palms. He wasn't sure if a leap of faith was something he could manage. The last time he'd tried it had been devastating. Only an idiot would chance going through that again. The likelihood of any relationship surviving in this day and age was statistically dismal. The odds were against success and pointed toward the same suffering he'd already been through.

Fuck. Not wanting to lose her warred with not wanting to get his heart torn to pieces, and he had no fucking clue which was the right choice.

"Morning." She kissed his shoulder, rolled over so that her back was to him, and cuddled her bottom into his hip. Her voice was sleepy and soft. "You wanna swim today?"

"In a little while." He turned and wrapped himself around her, wishing he could absorb some of her goodness, her honest joy in life. For all she'd been through, she'd managed not to become bitter. It was something he couldn't say for himself.

Burying his face in the crook of her neck, he breathed in her scent. His time with her was running out. It was important to savor every minute.

"I think I want to swim." She yawned, rubbed her eyes, but didn't try to get up.

He kissed her nape. "Are you even awake yet?"

"Um...kinda?" She shifted on to her back and reached over to stroke his jaw. "Caffeine would help."

He tried to keep his turmoil off his face when he looked at her. Savor the moment. Right. "A dip in cold ocean water is eye-opening too."

"Aw, that's mean." She tugged on his earlobe. "I wouldn't dump you in the Pacific without at least a cup of coffee first."

"Such a nice lady." He dipped down to brush his lips over the swell of one pert breast.

"Considering what we did in bed last night, I doubt anyone would call me a lady." She attempted a leer, but it just made him laugh.

He traced his fingertips in circles on her naked thigh. "Reminding me of what we did is not a way to convince me to go swimming."

"You're the one who got me hooked on sea swimming." She folded her arms, which plumped her cleavage. He nuzzled the soft globes and was rewarded with her shiver.

"I could talk you out of it." He moved his hand higher on her leg, his thumb just brushing the thatch of curls between her thighs. His body kicked to life, reacting predictably to her nearness. He could be half-dead and he thought he'd still respond for her.

She caught his wandering fingers. "Sex in the shower after? I want to swim with you."

"All right." He heaved an exaggerated sigh and flopped over onto his back. Desire still burned in his veins, but it wasn't at undeniable levels. Yet. She could make it up to him later. "I *guess* I could wait that long to have you."

"Such willpower." She widened her eyes at him. "You're such a strong man."

"Ha." He swatted her thigh. "Go put your bikini on before I test *your* willpower."

Rolling to her feet, she stuck her tongue out at him. "Right, like my crochet bikini doesn't make you drool."

"I do *not* drool. Drooling is so undignified." He arched a supercilious brow. "I do, however, get a serious boner."

She curved an arm over her belly and giggled. "Okay, then. You need to head back to your room to change. Meet me downstairs."

"Sure." After rising, he threw on the slacks and shirt he'd worn to the Royal Hawaiian the night before. He set up the coffeemaker so she'd have a fresh cup when she came out of the bathroom. Then he draped his jacket and tie over one arm and snagged his cell phone off the nightstand.

A few emails had come in since he'd last checked, so he tapped the screen to access the messages. The top email caught his attention. It was from Lilith. The air whooshed out of his lungs, and he sat down hard on the bed. He hadn't heard a word from her in all the years since his divorce and *now* she decided to get in touch? What could she possibly want? And did he really want to know? He stared at the screen for a full minute before he clicked on the message.

Lukas, I'm trying to sell the Toyota and the DMV says you're still on the title as co-owner. I thought you took care of this! We need to take your name off the car so I can get rid of it. I don't have your new phone number, so get back to me ASAP! -Lilith

He had to reread the note several times before he made sense of it. Then the burn of self-righteous anger filled his gut. He *had* changed the title on both cars when they'd separated. Of course, a fuckup by DMV was somehow his fault. It was her car and it had taken her five damn years to figure out his name was still on the title, but yeah, that was his fault. Because she was never wrong. If she was, she always found a way to lay the blame on someone else. That was how she stayed in control of every situation.

"You have to be fucking kidding me." His hand was trembling, and he had to clutch the phone tighter to keep from dropping it. Rage and sick helplessness churned in his gut.

Thank God he'd gotten out of that mess. Just reading her email was like having a black wave crash over him and swallow him whole. The past threatening to drag him back into hell just when he'd finally started letting in another woman. Of course, it had happened now. Fate was one nasty bitch, coming to shove his face in the reality of how badly relationships could go. They started with such promise but look where you ended up.

How could he ever have imagined that he could go back to that, open himself up to that kind of agony and suffering? He could feel himself spinning out, overreacting to the situation, but he was going to have to deal with this, which meant dealing with his ex and getting sucked back in to her morass of drama and accusations. Every muscle in his body was tense, so rigid he was shaking.

Hearing from her was the last thing he'd ever wanted. When their divorce had been final, he'd felt nothing but intense relief. But he'd suddenly been thrust onto that same old gut-wrenching emotional rollercoaster. Shit. Shit, shit, *shit*.

"Hey, I figured you'd be gone by now."

Julie's voice snapped him back to the present, and he jackknifed to his feet. "I...uh..."

"What's wrong?" She came toward him, concern in her brown eyes.

He backed up a step, and she stopped, confusion replacing the concern.

"Lukas, what's wrong?"

So much, and yet...nothing. Wasn't this his normal state of being? The scent of coffee singed his nose, so strong it was nauseating. He shook his head, trying to clear it. "I just got an email and I have some stuff I have to deal with."

"Crisis email, huh?" She didn't come any closer, but she offered a little smile. "Is there anything I can do to help?"

Yes, stop being so wonderful, so tempting, so everything he'd ever wanted in a woman and never thought existed. Stop all of that, and he'd be just fine. Instead of unloading his bullshit all over an innocent bystander, he cleared his throat and squeezed out, "No, this is something I have to handle myself."

"Okay, no problem." Her smile wavered, and she played nervously with the strap on her bikini—not the crochet one, thank God, but she looked amazing in anything. "I'll see you later, I guess."

He forced his gaze away from the temptation she presented. He should make this a clean break, walk away, not look back. His brain told him one thing, but his heart insisted something else. "Yeah...I guess. Though I don't think I'm up for anything today." He swallowed. "I have to go."

There was a long pause, and he expected her to say something cutting for his abruptness, but her voice dropped into low, understanding tones. "All right. Go do what you need to do."

Turning before he said something he couldn't take back, he strode out the door. When he got back to his room, he went hunting online for contact information for the California Department of Motor Vehicles. If he could get this straightened with them instead of having to deal with Lilith, that would be the best possible resolution. He hoped like hell that was possible.

Hope. *Ha.* There was a joke. And the joke was on him.

U neasiness twisted inside of Julie for the next few hours. She sat on one of the hotel's poolside loungers, Kindle in hand, but her thoughts were chasing themselves in circles. Something had been wrong with Lukas, no matter how he might have brushed her off. Seriously, *seriously* wrong. She didn't know why she was so sure about it, but her every instinct told her that email had been far worse than he'd let on. But who emailed bad news the morning after Christmas? They should all still be in holiday food coma.

Had someone died? Every tragic scenario she could imagine went through her head. His house burned down, or one of his students had had a terrible accident, or Stanford had fired him—could professors be fired?—or he had a secret baby mama. Okay, so maybe that last one was from the romance novel she was pretending to read, but it was a possibility, however remote.

"Is this seat taken?" a light baritone voice asked.

She glanced up and saw a good-looking blond man. He motioned to the empty lounger next to hers, though his gaze was focused square-ly on the way her bikini fit her breasts. She hadn't worn the crochet one, so there was no other reason for him to be looking. If he had approached her on her first day in Hawaii, she might have been in-terested, but now she was far too wrapped up in Lukas to want some other guy ogling her chest.

Before she could muster up a suitable response, Lukas's rough tones cut across the scene. "Actually, yes, it is taken."

Julie leaned sideways to see around Mr. Baritone, sliding her sun-glasses down her nose so she could get a look at her German. His accent was especially thick, which she'd learned meant he was upset or passionate about something.

There was a glimmer of jealousy in his gaze that she would have hated in most men, but considering his hasty departure from her room this morning, she was pretty thrilled to see right about now. He stared down the blond, who swallowed and beat a hasty retreat.

Julie shoved her sunglasses back up to cover her eyes. "So...did you get everything settled?"

He shrugged. "I just..."

"Yes?" She let her Kindle drop to her lap.

He heaved a sigh, scrubbing a hand over his hair. "It's been a crap morning, and I knew the day would be vastly improved if I spent it with you. I couldn't stay away." He glanced at her. "I'm sorry for being so curt this morning."

"Not a problem." She waited a beat, hoping he'd be more forthcoming about what was in the email, but he said nothing else. While it was nice that he came to her because he knew being with her would make his day better, she wanted more. She wanted to know what had happened, and why he might want to stay away. That didn't sound good at all. How far could she push? His expression was guarded, his body tense. Now wasn't the time to pry. Maybe after he'd loosened up a little. She drew her knees up to her chest. "What did you want to do today?"

"I was thinking..." For a moment, he looked as if he were groping for something to say. "Have you been up to Diamond Head yet?"

Somehow, she thought he had pulled that suggestion out of thin air. Weirder and weirder. "No, though I can see it from my room. Is it a hardcore hike up to the top?"

He sat down on the lounger beside her. "It's a little steep and uneven, but if you have some decent tennis shoes, you should be okay."

"I do." She searched his face but found no real indication of what he was thinking or feeling.

"Good." After pulling out his phone, he tapped a series of keys on the screen. "The eastbound bus leaves in about twenty minutes. Think you can hurry?"

He seemed almost jittery...like he knew he was doing something he shouldn't be. Which was strange because he hadn't acted that way the rest of the week and they'd spent every day together. What the hell was going on with him? She wanted to ask so badly, but reconsidered. He could refuse to answer and walk away the same way he had this morning. Better to wait until he was trapped with her on the bus or hiking up a mountain. Maybe it was devious, but she didn't have a lot of other options. This was the first time his reserved nature had left her on the outside looking in. She didn't like it at all.

"Twenty minutes? Easy peasy." She rose from her chair and grabbed her towel and e-reader. "Meet you in the lobby in ten. Less, if the elevators aren't crowded."

When she reached her room, she grabbed a T-shirt and a pair of shorts and slid them on over her bikini. Socks and sneakers completed the ensemble. Ready as she'd ever be. She was out the door in under three minutes.

Lukas was waiting in the lobby, bottles of water for the hike in each hand. He handed one to her and they hurried to the bus stop. It was just pulling up as they arrived, and they hopped on. Lukas leaned in to speak in her ear. "We'll only be on this bus for a couple of stops, then we transfer to the one we really need."

"Okay." She slipped her hand into his. He'd have to pull away if he wanted to keep up the emotionally distant routine. She knew what she wanted—*him*—and she wasn't about to pretend otherwise. Not when they had less than a day left together.

They got to the transfer point just in time to catch the next bus.

The few dark clouds in the sky opened up and it began drizzling lightly as they boarded. She laughed and fluffed out her damp hair. "Hawaii does like to catch me in the rain."

His eyebrow arched. "I remember."

"Fondly, I hope." She glanced back at him coyly.

"Very fondly. Your top was wet and clung to your breasts." The words were almost so quiet she missed them, but they brought a hot flush surging to her cheeks.

Unfortunately, the bus was crowded and she couldn't sit beside Lukas. So much for grilling him. It would have to wait until the ride home.

She would have guessed the volcano was farther from Waikiki Beach, but they arrived in twenty minutes. The hike up was a little more strenuous than she expected, the last third of the journey was up a set of stairs and through a tunnel that burrowed into the mountain. She definitely got her cardio in for the day. She could feel the burn in her thighs and glutes when they finally made it to the top.

But the view was worth it.

The vista was probably one of the most incredible she'd ever seen. They explored the rim of the volcano, but what struck her the most was the view of Honolulu. The rain had stopped and shafts of sunlight shot through the dissipating clouds, illuminating the ocean, beach, and green expanse of the island. If she didn't know better, she'd swear she was looking down on heaven.

"Wow," she said reverently.

"Reminds you how small people are in the grand scheme of things, doesn't it?" Lukas slipped his hands in his pockets, his gaze sweeping the horizon.

Downtown looked tiny, when the buildings had towered over her head a few days before. She took a breath and let it out. Aunt Eloise would have loved this view, would have insisted right up until her stroke that she could make that hike no matter what anyone else said. The thought made Julie smile.

She spread her arms wide, extending her fingers to let the breeze wash over her skin. It was good to be here, good to be alive and doing what she was doing. She couldn't ask for anything more. Maybe that meant her grief was finally starting to loosen its stranglehold on her heart. Life went on. She'd always miss Eloise, her mother, and everyone else she'd ever lost, but she had to embrace living again. She felt like she'd been a zombie the last year, just going through the motions without truly feeling any of it. Like her emotions were wrapped in a cocoon so thick nothing else could penetrate it.

Until now.

Maybe it had been getting away from everything, maybe it had been the electric connection of meeting Lukas, but something had jolted her out of her funk. It felt amazingly good. This was exactly what she'd needed. Perspective, distance, a chance to do nothing other than breathe, relax, and *exist*.

She let her arms drop and hugged herself. "This is paradise. I love it here."

"Planning to relocate?" Lukas turned his head to look at her.

"No, though I can see myself coming back for another trip some time. I still love Half Moon Bay, and my friends and business are there."

His lips twitched at the corners. "Your business where you make naughty bikinis."

"Among other things." She blew a raspberry at him. "Like sweaters and gloves and socks and scarves. Mostly I teach classes and make and sell yarn, though."

His squinted as if considering that. "I'm guessing your classes are more hands-on than mine."

"Yeah, no one has to sit through a lecture with me," she said in a superior tone. "Think of it more as a lab section. Only a three-week version of a lab section, but I do assign homework."

"Do they get graded?"

It figured he'd want details on how things were evaluated. Always the scientist. But it was nice to banter back and forth. He seemed to have relaxed a bit. She turned into him, slipping her arms around his waist. "No, you can't fail my classes. You just lose money if you don't show up. You may need to come back for tutoring if you're bad at it though."

His grin was all kinds of wicked. "I'd love to see you tutor someone on bikini crocheting."

"You're never going to let that go, are you?" Standing on tiptoe meant she could brush her mouth against his.

"Never." He nipped at her lower lip. "I'm going to have sexual fantasies about how you looked in that thing until the day I die."

"You plan to go out as a dirty old man, huh?"

"Sure, why not?" He threaded his fingers through her hair, and after a moment his smile slid away. His eyes darkened. "We should probably head back down."

"Sure." She linked her arm with his as they started walking to the stairs. "You seem sad, Lukas. Care to talk about it?"

He sighed. "I don't think it would help."

At least he didn't deny something was wrong. She wasn't sure how much that was worth, but it was better than him acting like she had a screw loose for thinking he was *off* today.

"You never know until you try." She glanced over her shoulder as they took the many steps down. "It made me feel better to talk to you."

His sigh was even heavier this time. "I got an email from my ex-wife.

There was a mix up at the DMV and somehow my name was left on the title for her car."

"And it took her this many years to figure it out?" Not that Julie checked the title paperwork for her vehicle very often, but still.

"Apparently. She wants to sell it and can't because my name is still listed as co-owner. It's just..." He shook his head. "Hearing from her threw me for a loop, and I *hate* that."

It sounded like the contact had affected him on a deep level, and a vicious, jealous knife twisted inside Julie's chest. She didn't want him deeply affected by anyone but *her*. Even if she had no real claim on him, she felt what she felt. Possessive. It was a struggle to keep her voice even. "So you still care about her?"

"*God* no." He sounded horrified, and the loud burst of his words echoed in the long cement tunnel through the volcano. "I honestly wish I'd never met her. Marrying her was the biggest mistake of my life, and her email today just rubbed my face in it." His laugh was harsh. "No matter what, there's no real escaping your past."

"Wherever you go, there you are." They reached the bottom of the steps, and she took his hand. Emotions crowded inside her, and she wasn't entirely sure what else to say. She'd never seen him this upset. Her usually unflappable professor had been hit hard and she wanted to take the pain away, even though it was impossible.

"Yeah." He squeezed her fingers so tightly it hurt. "I just want..."

He headed down the mountain, still gripping her hand, and she had to scurry to keep up. "You want?"

"Circumstances to be different." He hunched a shoulder in a shrug. "But they aren't."

His vagueness worried her. Was it just his divorce that he wished were different? Or were there other "circumstances" he wanted to change? She waited a few minutes before she spoke again. "Is there anything besides the email that's bothering you?"

The troubled look he shot her said she'd hit the nail on the head. "Yes, but it's not something I can discuss with you." He leaned in to kiss her forehead, the touch almost reverent. "It's our last day together, and I'd like to focus on enjoying it. Okay?"

"Okay." She sighed, knowing she wouldn't get more out of him right now. "Though, for the record, you can discuss anything with me."

"We'll agree to disagree on that." He ruffled her hair. She squeaked and ducked away, but he caught her close. "Careful, *mein Liebling*. The slope is steeper than you think."

She took the opportunity to press her lips to his, and she was rewarded with a slow, lingering kiss that curled her toes. He held her a little too tight, as if he never wanted to let her go. Or maybe that was wishful thinking on her part. A wolf-whistle broke them apart, and she grinned. "Hey, at least it wasn't the giggling girls."

He snorted. "With any luck, that group has headed home. Let's go before someone calls the police on us for public indecency."

"Aw, it was just a kiss. We weren't even copping a feel." The second she turned around, her foot slipped out from under her.

Her heart stopped, and Lukas grabbed her right arm, but she still landed hard on her left hip. Muddy water oozed through her clothes as she sat there, taking stock of any aches and pains. Nothing too bad, actually. Her damp backside was going to be the most uncomfortable part.

"Are you all right?" Lukas squatted beside her, running his hands over her to check for injuries.

"Yeah." She wrinkled her nose and let him pull her to her feet. "Well, it wasn't the steepness that got me, it was the wetness."

"You're sure you're okay?" A muscle in his jaw twitched, and he was pale around the mouth.

"I'm sure, hon, I promise." She tried swiping at her shorts, but they were soaked and dirt-smeared. "Well, that's gross. I don't think they'll let me back on the bus this way."

She shrugged fatalistically, unfastened her shorts and stripped down to her bathing suit. A little immodest for most places, but in Hawaii, she doubted anyone would look at her twice. Turning her shorts inside out so the dirt was contained, she then folded them and tucked them under her arm. Her bikini bottoms would dry fast enough, so she would be fine.

Lukas cupped his palm, tipped a bit of his water into it, and wiped the remaining mud from her leg. He even managed not to get any of the liquid on her shoes and socks. He inspected his work and nodded. "That should do it."

"Thanks. Ready to go?"

When he didn't respond, she glanced down at him. He had the strangest look on his face, then he huffed out a laugh and shook his head. "You're really not upset, are you?"

"Look, I don't sweat the small stuff. That's never been my thing, but after this year?" She snorted. "If I didn't have a meltdown over giving up a good job, relocating my entire life, changing careers, and losing one of the people I loved the most in the whole world, I'm sure as hell not going to freak out over a little mud, or a flat tire, or whatever."

He said carefully, "Some of the women I know would have been more than a little pissy about all those things."

"Shit happens. I'm not thrilled when it does, but dirt washes off, tires can be changed, and life goes on. Part of me coming here was about getting on with my life, and I think I'm ready. Or as ready as I'll ever be. Acceptance is kind of the key. You have to accept what you can't control, or it'll drive you crazy."

He made an odd choking noise. "You have no idea how right you are."

She propped a hand on her hip, sudden suspicion narrowing her gaze. "Would these women you're referring to include your ex-wife?"

"In a major way." He nodded.

"Well, I'm not her, and not all women flip over every little thing." And if he was shoving her into a category with a woman he wished he'd never met, he wasn't likely to want to date her when they got back to the mainland.

"So I'm learning." He offered her his hand, a small smile playing around his mouth.

She twined their fingers. "But if you're that worried about my crash landing, you can give me a massage later. To help me work out any stiffness."

"Sure." His grin widened.

He kept her hand securely in his the rest of the way down the trail, clearly intending to make sure she didn't fall again. Without any covering on her legs, a second fall was likely to scrape the hell out of her skin. Not her idea of fun, so she watched her step.

Once they were seated on the bus, she leaned in to whisper in his ear. "When we get back, want to come to my room and help me clean up?"

Fire burned in his gaze, so hot she thought it might scorch her. His fingers twitched as if he wanted to reach for her, but then stopped himself. "You don't have anything else you'd rather do on your last night in Hawaii? Maybe that sunset catamaran sail?"

"I like sailing. If that's what you'd prefer to do, I'm happy to go with you. But I'd rather do you." If this was their final evening together, then she wanted it to be a one to remember.

God, they were *leaving* tomorrow. The thought made her chest squeeze with pain. She didn't want this to end. She'd tried not to dwell on the looming deadline on their vacation, but they'd ticked down from days remaining to mere hours. Swallowing hard, she smoothed a hand down her hair.

She loved him.

How had it happened so fast? It was insane. No one fell in love in seven days. It was supposed to take months, years, but the connection had been immediate and deep. Undeniable.

With the weirdness of the day, she was even less confident than ever that he'd say yes to getting together back home, but she had to ask. She had to try. Even if it meant she went home with a bruised and battered heart. She might only have the courage to ask him for a simple date, but she wanted a whole lot more. If she were looking for a fresh start on her life, she'd like to have it with him.

Lukas would certainly be the best Christmas present she'd ever received.

CHAPTER TEN

H e was so fucking weak. Lukas sighed as he followed Julie up to her room. His ability to resist her was pathetic. He'd told himself to cut things off and walk away, but after he'd spent a frustrating morning on the phone with DMV, all he'd wanted was to be near her. It was so easy to unwind with her, to relax and laugh and look on the bright side. He wasn't very good at that himself.

When he'd gone downstairs, he'd fully intended to find some breakfast, maybe take a walk, or go swimming. Alone. But as if they had a will of their own, his feet had carried him toward the loungers Julie liked to lie on. She might not have been there, but she was. And some jackass had been hitting on her. Lukas had no right to be jealous, but he was. Jesus, he was an idiot. A masochist of the worst order. Using her to ease his pain was only going to make it harder to walk away from her. He'd come so close to unburdening himself about *everything* that had happened with Lilith, telling Julie how fucked up it had all gotten, and if they hadn't been in public where anyone hiking the volcano could listen in, he probably would have.

"Want to help me wash my back?" Her gamine glance lured him

like a Lorelei as she unlocked her door and walked into her room.

He followed her because there was no other choice. For as long as this trip lasted, he'd give in to his craving for her, but the minutes were ticking down. "Isn't it your legs that need washing?"

"There, too," she agreed. "I guess you'll have to conduct a full inspection, Professor. I'm sure you'll do a thorough job."

"I'll make a study of it."

She kicked off her shoes, pulled her shirt over her head and tossed it aside, then stripped out of her bikini as she walked to the bathroom. Her slender back and round buttocks were a view worth committing to permanent memory. He just stood there, staring at her because he could, because it might be the last time.

Arching an eyebrow, she glanced over her shoulder. "Coming?"

"Often and with great enthusiasm."

She laughed the way he wanted her to, though his chest was so tight with emotion he couldn't acknowledge, he was surprised he could still breathe. Shaking himself, he took out a condom, shucked his clothes and entered the bathroom. She was bent over adjusting the water. He groaned, the sound echoing in the small space. She looked back, her grin knowing. She wriggled her backside for him and his shaft hardened to the point of pain. Pulling the knob that sent water gushing from the showerhead, she hopped into the tub.

He sheathed himself with the condom, stepped in behind her, and slid the curtain closed. Water pelted down on them and filled the air with wispy steam. She turned to face him, her mouth opened to speak, but he didn't let her get a single word out. He took her lips in a soul-searing kiss. He wanted to lock in the flavor of her forever, so he'd never forget it. There wasn't a single second of this week he wanted to lose from memory. He put everything he felt but couldn't say in that kiss. There was so much he wanted with her, but he couldn't have it.

Not if he wanted to keep his sanity in the process.

His palms stroked over every damp inch of her that he could reach, trying to memorize the curves and planes of her figure. The water sealed their bodies together, made the glide of their flesh an erotic thrill. He wanted to take it slowly, but she had other ideas. Her fingers danced across his skin, robbing him of thought. When she cupped his balls, massaging the soft sac, he backed her up against the shower wall.

Lifting her so she could twine her legs around his waist, he groaned as he eased her down on his erection. She whimpered, her arms wrapping around his neck to hang on for the ride. He fitted his palms over her ass, holding her in place for his thrusts. There was nothing that felt as fantastic as being inside her, forging their bodies into one. The heated water slid in beads down their limbs, adding another layer to the sensations.

He shoved his tongue into her mouth with the same rhythm he used to penetrate her sex, and her thighs clamped tight on his hips, her heels digging into his buttocks to spur him on. Not that he needed any encouragement. There was no holding back from her. This was all he could give her, and he wanted her to scream his name in ecstasy before he was done with her. Pistoning his shaft into her sleek channel, he raced her for orgasm, pushing her hard and fast the way he knew she liked. He ground his pelvis into her sensitive little nub, and she bucked against him.

"*Lukas!*" She threw her head back against the wall, sobbing as she shook apart in his arms. Her nails dug into his shoulders, and her sex fisted on his length in pulses that ripped his control to pieces. He couldn't wait, exploding into her warm, giving body. His climax went on forever as she dragged everything out of him. But he didn't want it to end. He never wanted it to end, and there was no choice. There never had been. He groaned, the sound as much pleasure as pain and he pounded into her until she shuddered with completion again and buried her face in his shoulder.

They rested against each other, gasping in the steamy air. He didn't know how much time had passed before she stirred. Reluctantly, he let her regain her feet. They finished showering in silence, and he assumed she was as wrapped up in her thoughts as he was in his.

She shut down the water and climbed out first. He followed more slowly, grabbed one of the spare towels lying folded on the rack above the toilet, and rubbed the terrycloth over his body.

Julie let herself air dry while she ran a brush through her hair, her gaze meeting his in the foggy bathroom mirror. "So...I was wondering if you're available for dinner."

"Tonight? Of course." His grin was lopsided. "Maybe it's presumptuous, but I assumed we would be dining together."

"No, I meant..." She smiled nervously, played with the bristles on her brush. "I meant dinner when we get back to California."

He jerked as if she'd slapped him. For one heart-stopping moment, he wanted to say yes. To take what she offered and never look back, escape the past and all its doubts forever. But he couldn't. "I'm sorry. I can't. I—I thought you understood this was just for the week."

Her gaze dropped to the countertop, but not before he caught the gleam of tears in her eyes. An awful, crushing weight slammed down on his chest and he felt as if he were drowning.

Her lips trembled, but she didn't turn to face him. "Things have been so good between us. I thought...I hoped you felt the same way."

"Julie..." His fingertips brushed the back of her shoulder. He needed to touch her so badly he ached with it, wanted to draw her into his arms and try to soothe her pain. But he was the cause of that pain, and he had no right to offer comfort.

She closed her eyes. "Maybe you should go now."

"Julie, please. Try to understand." But how could she, when he'd never really told her anything about his marriage? Just that it was bad. A lot of people had bad marriages, including one of her friends. But there was bad and there was *bad*.

She set her brush on the counter with slow, deliberate movements. "Why?"

"Excuse me?"

"You've spent a week with me, and we've had a great time. You're too smart a man not to realize that we're good together, in and out of bed. We fit. That doesn't come along every day." She turned around to look at him, defiance and hurt molding her expression. "So why would a date be such a bad idea? It's not like I'm saying we should get married, I'm just talking about dinner back in the real world. It *shouldn't* be a big deal, but apparently it is. I want to understand, like you said. I want to know why you won't at least consider the possibility of continuing the awesome thing we have going here."

"My divorce..." How the hell did he say this? He's never told anyone about Lilith. Her family knew what had happened because they'd been there, but no one else. He didn't even know how to put it all into words.

"A lot of people have relationships after they divorce, Lukas." She shrugged. "Many of them even remarry."

He blew out a breath. "I know, but...I don't think I could ever be one of them. I promised myself I would never go through anything like that again. That meant never getting into a solid relationship again, never going down a path that might even hint at the possibility of marriage." He swallowed, trying to gather enough spit in his mouth to force out what he needed to say. "I know it sounds extreme, but my marriage *was* extreme, at least in the end. My ex-wife—Lilith—was not...stable."

Her tone was just as hesitant as his had been. "She had...mental health issues?"

He nodded, wrapping the towel around his waist. He didn't want to have this conversation naked. He already felt stripped bare as it was. "When we first got together, she was on the controlling side. She liked every little detail to be perfect. I understood that, since I like things *just so* myself."

Two strides took him out of the bathroom, and Julie followed him. But once he was in the bedroom he didn't know what to do with himself. Sit on the bed where Julie and he had made love so many times? No.

Julie slid on a nightgown and flopped down on the floor, her back against the bed. "But she got worse?"

He sat down beside her, gripping the towel tight so it wouldn't slip. "It became unhealthy. I managed to dismiss and ignore it for several years." He flashed a bitter, self-deprecating smile. "Hindsight is 20/20, right? It got to the point where I couldn't ignore it when I came home from a summer research trip and she'd found a spider in the kitchen cupboard, decided that meant the room was 'dirty,' put all the dishes in garbage bags in the middle of the floor and demolished the cabinets."

Confusion clouded her features. "Like...called in a contractor to redo the kitchen because of a bug?"

He snorted. As if anything had been so simple with Lilith. "I wish. When I got home, there was nothing but a sledgehammer resting against the wall where the cabinets used to be. She'd spent the summer eating take-out and had no idea why I was upset when I confronted her about the fact that we had no kitchen." He shook his head. "When I suggested that she might want to talk to a psychologist, she claimed that nothing was wrong. What she'd done was perfectly reasonable."

Julie shifted around to face him, her eyes round. "And she was serious?"

"Very." He sighed, pinching the bridge of his nose. He didn't want to talk about this, didn't want to relive it all, but Julie deserved to know why he couldn't be with her. He wanted to—God, he wanted to—but he couldn't.

"Then what happened?"

"Things went downhill from there. The more I insisted that she needed help, the more she decided that *I* was the problem. Every time I pointed out something that she did or said was more extreme than the situation warranted, she just got more stubborn about her way being the only right way. I even tried to get her parents to stage an intervention. That was a spectacular failure." He rubbed a hand over his eyes. His stomach churned, and his body tightened as the memories assaulted him. He'd been sure they'd have a good life together when he'd married Lilith and he'd been so wrong. How long had he lived with a crazy woman before he'd even noticed? "Our fights got uglier, as you can imagine. Soon *everything* was 'dirty,' including sex and anything that had to do with me. On the next trip I took—only a few days for a conference that time—I came home and our bed was gone. In its place were two twin size beds with nightstands separating them."

"Because you were too *dirty* to even share a mattress with." Julie's hand closed around his wrist, and he could feel the tremor in her fingers. Or maybe that was him shaking. "Oh, Lukas. I'm so...oh my God."

He looked at her, his voice dropping to an agonized whisper. "Do you have any idea what it's like to have someone you love think you're disgusting? That touching you makes them unclean? That you're no better than a *disease?*"

A little sob escaped her and she clamped her free hand over her mouth.

"After that, I asked for a divorce." He shrugged helplessly. "Living with her had become impossible, and I couldn't force her to seek help."

The sad thing was...he'd still loved her, still cared, still hoped she'd get better. There was that awful word again: hope. Bitter bile burned at his throat. Back then, he would have done anything she needed if she'd just been willing to work on the problem. Because that was what a husband was supposed to do. Be strong and supportive. He'd tried and he'd failed.

Julie scooted a little closer to him. "The day we met, you said the divorce was ugly."

"Oh, ugly is far too pleasant a word for our breakup." *That* was when the love had died and been replaced with something far less kind. He didn't think it had gone as far as hate, but loathing definitely came into the picture. "She moved out of the house, but came back while I was at work and stole things that my parents gave me, just for spite. The stuff wasn't worth anything except sentimental value, but she took it to get back at me for wanting a divorce. Then she argued over every single thing in the settlement because she didn't want me to have anything. *Dirty* people don't deserve to be treated fairly, or so she told me."

"Jesus," Julie whispered. "Did she ever get help?"

His smile was humorless. "About a year after everything was finalized, I found a box of her family's old photo albums, so I called her parents to see if they wanted them back. They thanked me and said yes. Her father told me that Lilith had been admitted to a mental institution by her doctor."

She made a startled little sound. "Wow."

"Yeah." He nodded. A headache began hammering at his temples, the weight on his chest growing heavier by the second. "That was the last I'd heard of her, until her email this morning. I'd really hoped never to hear from her again."

"I don't blame you." Julie slid her arms around him and burrowed against his chest. "I'm so sorry, Lukas."

He held her tight and felt tears burn the backs of his eyes. For the innocence Lilith had ripped away from him, and for what he was about to lose with Julie. "So...the idea of dealing with another relationship is...I can't do it, *mein Liebling*. I swore to myself I wouldn't do that again. It's emotional suicide."

"I would never—"

He pressed a palm to the back of her skull. "Lilith would have said the same thing when we first got together. I know that you're not like her, but what happened with her left way too many scars for me to risk it. I don't know how to trust a woman anymore. Hell, I don't know how to trust my own judgment when it comes to choosing a woman. So I'm not going to. I'm sorry." He squeezed her closer. "If it helps at all, in the five years since my divorce, you are the *only* woman who's made me second guess my decision never to get into a relationship again."

"It does help, and it doesn't."

"I'm sorry," he said again. "I wish..." He sighed, shook his head. "Wishing is pointless. I never meant to hurt you. That would be the very last thing I ever wanted."

"I wish too." A smothered little whimper burst from her, and he felt her tears splash against his chest.

If there was one thing this week with Julie had showed him without any doubts, it was that not all women he was attracted to were like Lilith. He'd worried about that for a long time. But Julie was sweet and easygoing and not at all controlling or controlled. Unfortunately, he was still the same man he had been when they'd met. He was still cynical about love and relationships and knew that getting into one would be a mistake. He could tell himself that going out a few times in California wouldn't hurt anything, but it would be a lie. He was already in over his head with her. The only thing saving him was the fact that their affair would be over when they left the island.

The problem was, Julie was not only the first woman to make him second guess his no-relationship policy—she was also the first woman to ever make him wish he were a different kind of man. Sure, he'd wished many times that his marriage hadn't gone south, that he'd never married or even met his ex, but he was a practical soul. The past couldn't be changed. He had to live with his mistakes. He'd looked at his situation, his history, and made the very practical decision that relationships were a risk he should never take again. He just wished he had never had to make that decision. He wished he were the kind of man who could claim a woman like Julie for his own and know that it would be fine in the end, but he'd felt that way before and look where it had gotten him.

No. He couldn't do it. He'd barely survived the last time; he wouldn't be able to do it again. Not even for Julie.

He was who he was. Nothing had changed. He just wished things were different.

He lifted her hand, pressed a lingering kiss to the back of it, then shoved his fingers into her hair and forced her head back so he could slant his mouth over hers. It was wild and desperate and tasted like goodbye. She sobbed against his lips, clutching him tight. Their tongues tangled, the kiss so fierce he tasted blood. Hers or his, he wasn't sure and he didn't care.

After tearing her mouth from his, she whispered, "Don't leave yet. Stay a little longer."

He nodded, recapturing her lips.

J ulie couldn't stop the tears from falling. She cried for him and what he'd survived, and for herself. She kissed him harder, wanting to absorb him into her skin. Nothing had ever felt so right or hurt so much. There was no changing his mind, no talking a man who'd been shackled to a madwoman into giving love another chance. In his place, she couldn't say that she wouldn't have made the same choice he had. But that didn't make her soul ache any less.

All she had left was tonight, and she was going to wring every last sensation she could out of it. His arms held her almost too tight. But he eased the pressure of his mouth on hers. His lips played over hers—a soft, gentle caress in direct contrast to his ironclad embrace. Somehow that made it all the more erotic and her insides melted. Her nipples beaded, thrusting into his chest.

He tumbled her back on the carpet, and she snapped her legs around his flanks, unwilling to allow even the slightest space to come between them. The nubby fabric of his towel stimulated her flesh. "Inside me. Please, I want you inside me."

"I need a condom." He looked around, then reached out to grab his discarded pants. He pushed himself up to kneel between her spread thighs. Ripping open the square foil packet, he let the towel drop.

She drank in the sight of him, rough satin skin over steely musculature. He was so strong on so many levels—stronger than even he realized, she thought. It made her love him all the more, even though it shattered her heart. She held her arms open for him after he slid the condom on, and he came down on her, pressing himself deep into her sex. She was still damp and soft from their last round of lovemaking, and he slid within her easily.

Propping himself on his elbows above her, he locked his gaze with hers, and she watched the conflicting emotions flash across his face. She saw the passion and the pain and a hundred other things she couldn't identify. Their bodies moved together as if they'd been made to fit each other, arch and twist, thrust and grind, every breath, every touch in complete sync.

He shifted his weight to the left, and drifted his right hand up her ribs until he could cup her breast. His fingers plucked at the tip, sending tingles radiating through her.

"I love your hands on me." She tried to smile at him, but the attempt crumpled before it could form. Her vision grew blurry, and she blinked the moisture away so she could see him, so she didn't miss anything.

His hips undulated and he changed angle. The head of his shaft hit just the right spot within her, which took her from slow burn to flash fire in seconds. Orgasm caught her by surprise, slamming into her. A cry ripped from her throat and she clutched him closer, holding onto him like a lifeline. Tears slid unchecked down her cheeks, and she rocked her body against his, wanting to draw this out. One, two, three more thrusts and he groaned, shuddering against her as he reached his own climax.

He crashed down on top of her and she hugged him. His weight on her was so sweet, something she'd never feel again. It was too soon, far too soon, when he sighed and shifted backward, sliding free of her body and leaving her utterly empty.

"I'll be back." He went to the bathroom and, after a minute, she heard the toilet flush. When he came out, he sat on the edge of the mattress.

He looked at her and she looked at him. Neither of them said a word. What was left to be said? Nothing would change his mind, and nothing changed the fact that they were fourteen hours away from getting on different airplanes.

She pushed herself up and maneuvered until she sat beside him, her head pressed to his shoulder. Holding on to him felt like trying to tighten her grip on sand. He just slipped through her fingers faster. Her heart thudded painfully in her chest, and she realized if this was the end, she had one thing left she had to say to him, or she'd regret it forever.

"I love you, Lukas."

"*Julie.*" Her name was almost a sob on his lips. "Please...don't. You're killing me."

She nodded, pressing her trembling lips together. "I'm sorry. I just had to tell you while I still had the chance."

His big body shook, his hands clenching into fists. "I can't be in a relationship with you."

"Too late." She kissed his cheek, then whispered in his ear, "You're already in one. You just can't admit it, and I love you anyway." The hairs at the nape of his neck ruffled as her breath rushed out in a hitching little laugh. He leaned into her as if he craved her touch, but he didn't reach for her, didn't try to hold her. He was letting her go, and there was nothing she could do about it. If her love wasn't enough, nothing would be. It sucked so fucking bad. "Goodbye, Lukas. I'm sorry for what you've been through, but I can't regret the amazing, wonderful man you are. I hope someday you find someone who makes you toss that no-relationship rule out the window. I just wish it could have been me."

With that, she rose and walked into the bathroom. She heard the hotel room door open and close, and knew he was gone. She pressed her back to the wall and slid down in a heap on the cool tile floor. Drawing her legs up, she sobbed against her knees, letting all the pain and hurt out.

That was it. Done. Over.

She'd loved every minute she'd spent with him. Even with the mudslide down the volcano, the popped tire, and the bad traffic. Shit happened, but nothing had put a damper on this vacation. She'd come looking for peace, for closure, and she'd found that, but she'd found so much more. Love. Not fleeting, vacation infatuation either, but the real kind that she thought could last. Maybe a lifetime.

But the problem with love was that if it wasn't reciprocated, it wasn't worth much. Just a boatload of heartache. She'd lost so much already, she wasn't sure how she was going to survive this. Not that she had a choice. That was the thing about losing people you loved—it just happened, no matter what you wanted or how you might fight against it.

They were just gone.

CHAPTER
ELEVEN

Julie had thought losing her Auntie Eloise had been bad, but it was *nothing* to losing Lukas. Eloise had been taken by death, but Lukas was still alive and well and only a half hour away. But she still couldn't have him in her life. She'd been home for two weeks and she'd just been going through the motions. It was easier to be at Purl Moon than it had been before she'd left—the time away had given her the perspective she needed to get a handle on her grief. Mission accomplished, but she still felt like crap. Her heart *ached* in her chest, just for an entirely different reason this time.

The weather had turned cold and rainy, reflecting her mood perfectly. But the bad weather meant business in her shop was slow and no one was around to distract her. The morning was spent reviewing inventory, which wasn't the most thrilling part of the job, but it needed to be done and the familiarity of it helped her settle. Lunchtime rolled around, but she didn't feel like eating. She'd had a craving for Hong Kong buns and pineapple floats since she'd been back, and nothing else seemed to satisfy her.

When Anne's ring tone blared out of her phone, she leaped for it gratefully. Her friends knew what was going on, if only because Meg had taken one look at Julie when she'd gotten off the plane and it was all over. Meg knew something was wrong. Without a word, she'd opened her arms for a hug and Julie had started crying all over again.

Julie stabbed the button to accept the call. "Hey, Anne. What's up?"

"Hey, doll," her friend returned. "Do you want company or want to be left alone?"

Damn, if even Anne was being courteous and not barging into her shop to drag her out, she must have seemed worse than she thought. She took a sip of the chamomile tea sitting at her elbow. "I'd take some company. Just the girls though."

The idea of being hauled back to Anne's chaotic house for a visit was daunting. Two of her three younger sisters were home from college for winter intersession. Julie might be at loose ends, but no one was that desperate for company.

"Don't worry. I won't bring my sisters." A beat passed. "Or my mother, of course."

Julie almost spit out her tea. "I'd take your sisters over your mother any day."

"Who wouldn't?" Julie could all but see Anne roll her eyes. "Mom's going into Victorian decline because Cami's break is ending and she's going back to the dorms."

"Oh Jesus." Anything the drama mama could find to wig out about, she would. It wasn't like she'd done the raising of her daughters anyway. Anne had brought up the younger ones after her dad passed away.

"Tell me about it," Anne groaned. "I need to get out of the house for a while."

"How's Karen handling the Victorian decline?"

Anne was quiet for a long moment. "She went apartment hunting this morning. She's moving back to Half Moon Bay."

The announcement made Julie blink. Seriously? She'd broken up with Tate maybe sixteen *days* ago. "She didn't tell us she was house hunting."

Anne's sigh crackled the phone line. "She didn't tell anyone until she was on her way out the door. But you know how Karen is when she makes up her mind."

"Stubborn as a terrier. I'm just surprised she's moving so fast. I kind of expected them to try to work it out, maybe get some counseling." Then again, she wasn't sure if Tate had actually accepted that Karen had a legitimate beef with his workaholic tendencies.

And thinking about Karen's divorce made her think of Lukas and his ex-wife, and all the former spousal issues that kept people from moving on with their lives. She hoped Karen managed to get over Tate faster than Lukas had his ex. She knew that wasn't really fair, but it *hurt* to know you'd found Mr. Right and couldn't have him because of the former Mrs. Wrong. A tiny part of her kind of wanted to knock Lukas's and Tate's skulls together.

"He's an idiot for letting her go." Emotion choked those words, and Julie knew she'd taken Karen's news a little too personally.

Anne would have noticed too, but she didn't say a word. It might be the first time in her life that she'd managed to be circumspect about anything. "So, Karen wanted to meet for lunch at the Moonside Café. Meg said she could make it, and it looks like you can too."

"I might be more into coffee than food, but I'll be there."

"Do I need to nag you about eating right post-breakup?" Anne's tone turned threatening, and Julie's lips curled in a reluctant grin.

"When are we meeting?" She glanced at the clock. It was almost one.

"In thirty minutes."

Meg, Anne, and Julie sat at the Moonside Café half an hour later, waiting for Karen to finish up at an apartment tour. The waitress brought them a round of coffee without being asked. There was a sign that they'd been here once or twice. A week. For years. The familiarity of it felt nice, but it also felt...odd. Like trying on an old sweater. The fit was good, but Julie had changed so much since the last time she'd worn it. She'd have to readjust.

"You're not eating right, and I'm betting you're not sleeping well." Anne gave her a frank look. "Want me to hunt him down and kill him?"

Straggling out a laugh, Julie shook her head. "It's a tempting offer, but no. I understand why he didn't want to take our affair beyond Hawaii. I think...he had deeper feelings for me than he was comfortable with, and that made him even more reluctant to pursue anything with me. It scared him."

"Maybe he'll come around. I did." Meg's grin was sheepish. She'd put Finn through hell before she'd finally agreed to go out with him.

Julie shrugged, refusing to let herself give in to that kind of thinking. That would drive her batty. "Maybe, but I can't spend my life hoping, you know?"

Her friends exchanged a glance. Anne finally asked, "Do you love him?"

"Yeah." The word emerged as a sigh.

She'd been in love before, but nothing had ever felt so intense, so deep, so necessary. Yet it was...comfortable. Many of her other relationships had made her feel as if she had to alter some part of herself in order for it to fit. The time she'd spent with Lukas had been effortless.

Even when things were going wrong, they'd worked together to fix the issue and managed to laugh along the way. What heterosexual woman wouldn't want to hang on to a guy like that? Not counting his ex, of course, but she'd been mentally ill, so that had to be factored in.

Getting over Lukas was going to take a long, long while.

But she'd survive. It would hurt, but she'd get through this the way she'd gotten through everything else. One minute at a time, and every day would get a bit easier. She was strong enough to deal with this. She'd cry and be sad and get mad and vent to her friends, but life would go on. It always did.

The bell over the door jangled as Karen pushed through. She brushed her blonde hair out of her eyes, and managed a weak smile when she saw them. Man, Julie hoped she didn't look as bad as her friend. It was an uncharitable thought, but Karen looked like hell. Dark circles under her eyes, pinched features, pale cheeks.

"Hey." Julie held out her arms, and Karen came over to collapse in the chair next to her, leaning in for a hug.

A sudden little sob shook Karen's frame. "Men suck."

"They really, really do," Anne agreed.

Julie whispered, "I'm sorry he hurt you."

"Back at ya." Karen pulled away and swiped at her eyes. Her chin tilted defiantly. "Men. Boil them in oil."

Grinning wickedly, Anne leaned her elbows on the table. "We should have an anti-man party."

Shooting the redhead a glance, Meg was the one who dared to question the hating party. "What would that entail?"

Taking on her customary role of instigator, Julie waved a hand. "*Kill Bill* marathon? Sweatpants and sloppy hair. All the foods they tell you not to order on dates. More cupcakes than you can eat in a week."

"Ice cream?" Karen asked plaintively.

Meg pointed out, "It's January."

"With *hot* fudge sauce." Karen folded her arms over her chest and arched an eyebrow.

"Whatever you want."

The planning for the anti-man party had reached outrageous and ludicrous proportions, and it wasn't until Meg flatly refused to allow Finn to be used as the sacrifice on a makeshift altar that they'd decided to stick to fattening foods and bad movies. Julie was still grinning when she went back to her shop an hour later. The rain let up a bit, and she had a knitting class at four o'clock, so she was feeling a bit more cheerful than she had that morning.

Hanging out with her friends had been restorative. It had taken going away to realize how lucky she was. Not that she hadn't appreciated her life before, but she felt as if some of the burdens that had pressed down on her chest had dissipated in the time she'd been away.

She spent some time processing online orders, prepping shipments of yarn, and catching up with paperwork. It felt good to check things off the to-do list. She wandered around the store, straightening and organizing as she went. Her gaze went to the roving yarn in the basket next to her spinning wheel. The last batch she'd dyed with Auntie Eloise, still unfinished. A sad smile curved her lips. She wondered what Eloise would have made of Lukas. Julie thought the old lady would have approved. She definitely would have approved of an island love affair. Of course, Auntie would have focused on the affair, where Julie focused on the love.

Drawing in a deep breath, she went over to the wheel and sat down. She needed to finish this batch. For her aunt, for herself, to prove how far she'd come. It was time. She was ready.

It occurred to her that without Lukas to listen and understand and offer comfort, she might not be in a mindset where she could say a final goodbye to this last project. He'd given her so much—probably more than he'd realized—and she'd always be grateful for that. The rest would take time and acceptance and patience, but she'd be okay. Some day.

"Professor, I think I figured out the problem we discussed."

Lukas glanced up from his computer at one of his graduate student assistants. The young man had his laptop in hand and a flush of excitement to his cheeks. The thrill of new discovery. Then again, this particular student tended to be excited about everything. He had the endearing and obnoxious personality of an overeager puppy.

"Come in." He waved the student into a chair, and they spent the next hour and a half working through the research the student was assisting him with. They made good progress, and Lukas sat back satisfied.

"These are some truly exciting results, Dr. Klein. I can't wait to finish work on the article so we can share our findings." His eyes widened. "This is just mind-boggling."

Lukas looked away to hide his grin at the quiver of eagerness in the young man's voice. "We've done good work here, but we have a great deal more to do."

"But that's the best part! Don't you just love your work?"

"When politics don't get in the way, yes. I really do." Lukas nodded, rose, and started packing his leather messenger bag. It was time to wrap up for the day.

The student's feathery eyebrows rose. "Politics?"

"Doctorate means ego and a university is full of them." Lukas shrugged.

"Doctorates or egos?" The student rolled his eyes. "Yeah, both. Well, I'll avoid the politics as long as I can and continue to relish my work. I'll email you as soon as this last set of simulations is complete."

"You do that."

The young man bounced to his feet, shook Lukas's hand with enough vigor to dislocate his shoulder, and then scurried out of the office. Yes, definitely an overeager pup.

He grinned and shook his head. Julie would crack up and make comments about housebreaking the grad students when he told her ab—

The thought cut off before it even finished. He couldn't tell Julie anything. In fact, he didn't have anyone to tell about this. One of his colleagues, perhaps. His mother, when he called her on Monday. But there was no one to talk to when he got home tonight.

Sure, he was alone. By choice. He'd been alone since his divorce, but this was the first time he'd noticed he was also *lonely*. His house was empty and didn't have half the life that those two small hotel rooms in Hawaii had offered. Because he'd shared them with Julie.

The longer he'd gone without her, the more he'd questioned the decision he'd made. Had it really been wise not to conduct that particular relationship experiment? To not even *try?* If he had given up at the first challenge he'd ever faced, he wouldn't have made it through graduate school or survived the shark-infested waters of the tenure process.

The problem was, his last relationship was the most traumatizing thing that had ever happened to him. Overcoming that was more of a challenge than he'd ever faced before. He'd just never found anyone or anything that made it worth it to him.

Until now.

After flipping off the light switch and locking up his office, he headed for his car. The last two weeks had forced him to do a lot of soul searching.

He'd exchanged a few more emails with Lilith about the car in order to arrange things so she could sell it. Somehow, dealing with her now didn't seem as big an issue as it once had. She was the past and, for the first time, he knew that was true instead of just paying lip service to it. She'd been a sad, troubled woman and didn't seem to have changed much, despite her stint in an institution, which made her all the more pitiable. He hadn't been able to see that clearly when he'd been hip-deep in the drama of her problems, but he could now. He hoped for her sake she got some real help someday, but that wasn't his concern anymore. Still, he was thankful he hadn't had to see her or speak to her to get the vehicle issue straightened out. Less contact was better. He had no desire to get sucked back in to the quagmire that was Lilith. But he didn't loathe her anymore. She was a sick woman and that wasn't his fault. He'd done his best by her, but he couldn't save her from herself. He wasn't to blame for that either.

He really had managed to get beyond what his marriage had done him. Who'd have thought it possible? And he could lay the credit at Julie's feet. He wasn't the same man he'd been before he met her. She was like a storm that broke over his life and swept everything along in its wake. It wasn't until the storm passed that one could assess the changes that had been wrought.

He loved her for it. He loved her for being her, for accepting and understanding him, for...everything. And he hadn't even had the guts to tell her before he left. It was the one thing he truly regretted about their time together.

The sky was just starting to turn pink and orange with sunset when he reached the parking lot. It wasn't as lovely as the ones in Hawaii, but he wouldn't have cared if he had Julie by his side. And that was exactly where he wanted her.

So what was he still doing here, thinking about how much he owed her, how much he missed her, how much he *loved* her? She was only thirty minutes away if he got in his car and headed west.

He'd been asking himself the same question for three days now, and the bottom line was he was scared shitless. What if he finally got up the nerve to try again and then she rejected him? She had every right to. He'd refused her love and walked out on her. He deserved it if she wanted to punch him in the face. It had never been his intention to hurt her, but he'd done so anyway. And now he had to figure out how to make it right.

No small task for a man who'd been running scared from women like her for five years. And he honestly couldn't say he regretted it. If he'd settled for someone else after his divorce, he might never have met Julie. And that would have been the real tragedy.

"Shit." He flung his bag onto the passenger seat of his car and then slid in behind the wheel. He dug out his cell phone, pulled up her number, and stared at it. Just as he had for the last three days. What would he say to her? That he was an ass and she could do better than a bitter, used-up jerk like him? That he loved her and would worship the ground she walked on for the rest of his life if she would just stay the amazing woman she was and never go crazy on him? Hell, all of that. And it felt wrong to have that conversation over the phone.

He tapped the screen and exited his contact list. On impulse, he did a search for fiber arts stores in Half Moon Bay. Three came up and he remembered hers was called Purl Moon. It was open until 7pm today. It was 6:15pm now.

Just enough time to get there, if he hurried. Sliding the key in the ignition, he blew out a breath. He needed to *see* her, not just call her. So he started his car and drove. Traffic was light and there was a parking space open right in front of her shop. If he were the type to believe in fate, he'd say it was a sign.

His fingers trembled a little as he reached for the door handle to Purl Moon. What if the place were loaded with customers? What if she didn't want to see him? He'd pushed her out of his life, rejected the love she'd offered so freely.

He'd made her cry.

That was the worst crime of all. He'd had heaven within his grasp and he'd been too stubborn, too blind, and too gutless to hold onto it. She might see that as unforgivable, no matter how he tried to justify his actions. She knew his reasons, but she also knew he'd stomped all over her heart.

Closing his eyes, he swore under his breath, grabbed the handle, and walked inside. The place screamed of Julie. Beautiful, quirky, and something about it just made you want to reach out and touch. There were yarns tucked into every nook and cranny. Diamond shaped shelves laddered up to the ceiling, all stacked with bundles in a myriad of colors. There was a babble of voices coming from the back, so he followed the sound, unsure if he was happy or not that someone else was clearly here. It meant someone else would witness whatever happened next, but it also meant she might not throw him out the moment she saw him. She wouldn't want a customer to see a confrontation.

And there she was, so beautiful she made him ache. She spoke with two elderly women, discussing the difference between soy and bamboo. Soy yarn, really? He slid his hands in his pockets and allowed himself the simple pleasure of watching her. If this didn't go well, it might be the last time he got the opportunity. The other women turned away and began packing up their belongings, and it was now or never.

"Julie."

Her head snapped up, her eyes rounding with shock as she stared at him. "Lukas."

She took a step toward him, then hesitated and he didn't know if that was a bad thing or a good thing.

"Is this a friend of yours, dear?" one of the old ladies piped up, her blue eyes gleaming with interest behind her thick glasses.

"Who cares if he's her friend?" her companion bellowed the way only the mostly-deaf could. "He's got an ass like two scoops of French vanilla ice cream."

"Please, Trudy." The first woman flapped a dismissive hand. "You can't even see his butt. He's facing us. You need your prescription checked."

Trudy barked out, "Well, turn around, boy, and let us see your ass."

He looked to Julie, uncertain how to react. But she was bent over at the waist, a hand clamped over her mouth, and tears ran down her face as her shoulders shook with silent mirth. The wretch. So he turned around and let the old ladies ogle his ass. What the hell? It wasn't like this was going to be a comfortable encounter anyway, and he had a feeling it might make—

He smiled when Julie let loose with ringing peals of laughter. God, he'd missed that sound. His chest cinched so tight with emotion, it threatened to strangle him. Turning back, he arched his eyebrows with a nonchalance he didn't feel. "Did I pass inspection?"

Trudy grinned lasciviously. "Two scoops. Yum."

"Thank you." He tried for a gallant bow, but figured he looked like jackass.

Julie clapped her hands together. "All right, ladies, you're going to be late for bingo night if you don't get going."

"I'm driving," Trudy bellowed.

Her friend snorted. "In your warped, twisted little dreams. My ride, I drive."

"Good night!" Julie ushered the geriatrics out the door and locked up.

Lukas's palms were sweating by the time she returned. The moment of truth. Too bad he had no idea what to say. How did you convince the most amazing woman you'd ever met to forgive you for having a hang-up or twelve about relationships?

So he went for the most mundane question he could come up with. Profound was beyond him at the moment. "How are you?"

She huffed out a breath. "Brokenhearted. Last month, I got dropped by the man I loved. It kind of sucks, you know?"

His heart stuttered. "Loved, past tense?"

"What are you doing here?" She crossed her arms over her chest, her chin jutting stubbornly. Both a defensive and defiant gesture in one.

"I missed you." He tried to smile and guessed it probably looked more like a grimace. "I've been brokenhearted without you."

Her lips compressed. "That was your choice."

"I was an idiot." He swallowed. "Julie, I..."

She shook her head, holding up her hands as if to ward him off. "Lukas, unless you've completely changed your mind about a relationship, you really can't come here. I really can't take it."

"I've changed my mind," he rushed out before she withdrew that offer.

Moisture glutted her eyes, and she rolled them. "Why? You were pretty damn sure of your decision two weeks ago. What changed?"

"I did."

"Excuse me?" She sniffed, blinking quickly before the tears could fall.

"*I* changed." He took a step toward her and was relieved when she didn't back away. Her eyes were still wide and shadowed with doubt and pain, but she was listening. He took another step. "Knowing you changed me. The longer we were together, the more I wanted to get beyond the crap from my divorce. I thought avoiding relationships would spare me that kind of heartache again, and it did, but it also left me alone in life. Which I didn't mind so much, until you."

Her hands balled in the hem of her sweater and a single teardrop slipped down her cheek. "Oh really?"

His stomach clenched at the sight of that droplet of moisture. "Yes, really."

One corner of her mouth tilted upward. "So, this means you'd be willing to have dinner with me?"

"I want a lot more than dinner, Julie." At her wicked smirk, he shook his head. "I'm not talking sex, though I want that too. I want something *real* with you."

Her eyebrows scrunched together. "I'm not convinced you're ready for that."

That was fair, considering everything he'd said to her on the island. But for the first time in a long time, he wasn't running away from anything, or trying to protect himself from pain. He was trying to reach for something *good*. "You know, from the first day we met, I thought about seeing you after we got home. I decided against it because I knew—I *knew*—that there was never going to be anything casual with you. Even at the beginning, you made me *feel* things I hadn't felt...ever."

Sympathy reflected in her gaze. "With everything you'd been through, I'm guessing that scared you."

"Damn straight. The only way I let myself touch you in the first place was because there was a time limit." He rubbed the back of his neck. "No, that's not true. That was the excuse I gave myself. I wouldn't have been able to keep my hands to myself no matter what. You were...irresistible."

The corners of her eyes crinkled. "Back at you. Though I wasn't trying to resist."

"I love you."

Her smile slid away as if it had never been, her face going pale. Her mouth opened and closed, but no words emerged.

"I love you, Julie." There, he'd said it. Relief filtered through him. He didn't have to fight it or pretend he didn't feel it. It was out in the open. He took a final step toward her, and now he was close enough to reach out and cup her cheeks. "I love you so damn much. I didn't mean to fall for you, I didn't even want to, but I'm glad I did."

"Lukas." His name came out soft and breathy.

Two more silvery tears streaked from her eyes. He caught them with his thumbs, wiped them away.

Her mouth twisted with uncertainty. "How do you know that this won't go wrong like it did before? You said that, in the beginning, your ex would have told you she wouldn't hurt you either."

"I don't know it won't go wrong," he returned. It still terrified him, but the thought of never seeing her again, never talking to her, never touching her, petrified him even more. "There's no way to know for sure. It's a risk, an experiment. Sometimes those lead to stunning new discoveries and sometimes they blow up in your face. But you're worth the risk. No one has ever clicked with me the way you do, on every level. I tried to walk away, but my heart wouldn't let me. I love you."

She closed her eyes. "I don't think I'm ever going to get tired of hearing you say that."

"Good." Swooping down, he took the opportunity to kiss her

lightly. The sweet flavor of her made him shudder with a need that was as emotional as it was physical. He needed this woman more than he needed air to breathe.

Her hands pressed to his chest. "We can take this slowly, you know. There's no need to rush into anything. Dinner or sailing or just hanging out. No one's running down the aisle or committing to anything other than being together and loving each other. That's the most important part to me anyway."

"Me too." He wrapped his arms around her and hauled her against his chest. Right where she belonged. His eyes slid closed as he savored the feel of her. Nothing had ever felt so damn right in his entire life.

She slipped her fingers into his hair. "I love you."

"I love you too."

Then she pulled him down and their lips met and they didn't talk for long, long minutes. He slid his tongue along her lower lip, dipping in to explore her mouth. It had been weeks since he'd had the opportunity, and he meant to enjoy it. He let his hands drift down her back, and she pressed tighter to him. Her breasts against his chest, her thighs against his hardening erection, every inch of her fit perfectly in his embrace. Her fingers clenched in his hair, and she twined one leg around his thigh. Rocking into her did nothing to assuage his need, but he relished the burn of anticipation.

She released his mouth, smiling up at him. "I missed this. I missed you."

"I've never been so lonely in my life." Resting his forehead against hers, he met her gaze. "Your website said your shop doesn't open until ten tomorrow."

She raised her eyebrows. "Yeah...and?"

"Want to see what's playing at the Stanford Theatre tonight? And then have a sleepover at my place?" He smoothed his palms over her backside, pulling her tighter against his erection.

She arched into him, making him groan. "And try the crack sprinkled popcorn? How could I resist?"

He laughed, and it felt good. He kissed her again, and it felt even better. He loved her, and that was the best part of all. Who knew what the future held? For right now, he was just happy to be holding Julie. If he took this one day at a time, maybe it wouldn't be quite as terrifying. Add enough days together and it would be fifty years later and Julie would still be laughing in his arms.

Now that was something worth getting his hopes up for.

THE END

Up next in this series is Karen and Tate's reunion story. Want a sneak peek at how they got together? Join C. Jordan's mailing list for a FREE copy of the bonus short story, *Just This Once.*
https://www.cjordanbooks.com/bonus-content/

ABOUT C. JORDAN

C. Jordan is a California native with an insatiable love for travel. When she's not writing sexy contemporary romance, she can usually be found working as a librarian or wandering the world with her husband.

ALSO BY C. JORDAN

EXCErpT From MaYBe THIS TIME

Half Moon Bay, California

"**S**o, are you going to change your last name back to Hudson?" Ben asked.

Karen froze at the question from her younger brother. A group of her closest friends and their siblings had come over to her new apartment to help her move in and unpack. They all knew why the move was happening, but only Ben had the temerity to ask about her imploding marriage. Even her friend Anne, who was usually as in-your-face as a person could get, had had the graciousness not to probe that wound too deeply. And if Anne was being circumspect, you knew it was bad.

"Jesus, Ben, really?" Nora—one of Anne's three quirky younger sisters—punched him in the shoulder.

"What?" His brows snapped together and he rubbed his arm. "It's an honest question. It's not like I didn't ask her how she was doing and everything."

She rolled her eyes. "Still, that's really what you want to ask immediately after your sister"—her voice dropped to a whisper loud enough to be heard two counties over—"files for divorce? You're so sensitive."

"You're so sensitive," he fired back. "No wonder you're a psych major. You have to feel your feelings about every damn thing."

She flushed scarlet and jammed her hands down on her hips. "I switched my major to nursing, jackass."

Ben already had his mouth open to retort, so Karen figured it was time to wade into the fray. Those two had been at loggerheads since junior high, and it showed no sign of stopping even though they were both in their mid-twenties. "Okay, guys. Knock it off or I'm giving you a time out and making you stand with your noses in separate corners."

Anne snickered from where she knelt on the living room floor amidst a sea of half-empty boxes. Their other best friends, Meg and Julie, ducked their heads in from the bedroom.

Julie said, "I'm so glad I'm an only child."

Meg elbowed her in the ribs. "Uh...where do you want us to stick the sweaters and winter clothes?"

Not to be denied his parting shot, Ben turned back to Nora. "Besides, what was I supposed to do? Talk about the weather?"

Sighing, Nora shook her head as if his stupidity saddened her. "Sure, that would have worked better. But maybe tell her that her hair looks awesome instead of reminding her about...stuff."

Stuff being the breakup, the divorce, the end of life as Karen had known it for the last eight years. Stuff being where she went from being Mrs. Tate Patton to Ms. Karen Hudson again. Nope, she absolutely did not want to talk about that. So she fluffed the textured layers of her recently shortened crop. Her once shoulder-length blonde hair now ended just below her chin, and instead of straightening it to perfection as she'd been doing for years, the mussed style took advantage of her natural wave. Maybe the hair reflected the new Karen, because she was tired of pretending to be perfect—that her life was perfect, that cool, calm perfection was even something she wanted. A little muss was just fine with her.

"It really does look nice, sis. Totally different." He winked. "I'm guessing that's what you wanted."

"Yep." To prevent further outbursts between Nora and her brother, she gave him a smile. "Why don't you go down to the moving truck and see if Finn and Lukas need a hand with the heavy lifting? Leave the unpacking to us."

Finn and Lukas were Meg's and Julie's boyfriends, both of whom had been roped into helping and hadn't complained once about the unpaid labor. It made this day both easier and harder that everyone was being so nice and tiptoeing around Karen's feelings. She was just happy her parents were out of town on an extended vacation—them being here adding their quiet sympathy and support to everyone else's would have made it that much worse.

"I'm happy to assist in the estrogen-free zone." Ben was out the door in seconds, though he cast a baleful glance back at Nora before he disappeared.

Nora snorted. "Estrogen-free zone, my ass. No wonder he doesn't have a girlfriend. He's probably still a virgin because he can't be *nice* long enough to get laid."

"Whoa!" Karen slapped her hands over her ears. "I do not want to speculate about my brother's sex life."

"Or lack thereof," added Anne. She gave her sister a pointed look. "Now who's being insensitive?"

"Heh. Me." Nora's grin was abashed. "Sorry, Karen."

Karen was thankfully spared further discussion when Anne's other sisters, Hazel and Cami, tromped in with Chinese food for lunch. Not that things were likely to settle down upon their arrival. The sisters together in the same room was often like fire, gasoline and a dry forest just waiting to explode into flames. Anne played referee with that trio so often she could go pro.

"Put the bags on the table, girls." Karen cleared a spot wide enough for the multitude of white cartons. "And go call the guys."

Her brother would have to come back to the estrogen minefield, but he'd need to brave it if he wanted to get fed.

Meg fetched paper plates and Anne rooted around in the boxes until she came up with a set of mismatched silverware. It wasn't the sleek, expensive set Karen and Tate had gotten as a wedding present, but Karen was just as happy not to have the reminder of all her dreams turning to dust.

She tried to paste on a smile for everyone, but it got harder as the day progressed. All her belongings were unpacked and put away. Her new life was in order. She even had a job lined up as director of the Half Moon Bay Public Library. A step up from assistant director at the main library in Palo Alto. She started in two weeks. Everything was going smoothly, so she shouldn't have any complaints.

But how could she feel happy about the dissolution of the life she'd wanted so badly? She'd had something so amazing and wonderful in her grasp, but it had soured and she'd had to let it go or turn sour herself. That didn't mean she was happier for the loss.

If only Tate had—

No, she wasn't letting that awful merry-go-round spin in her head again. They'd been in sync when they'd married, but had grown apart, had wanted different things. She'd wanted a family and had let him put it off until he finished law school, until he'd established his career, until he'd made partner, but eventually she'd realized that he just didn't want what she wanted, no matter what he might claim. He wanted to be married to his job, and she couldn't compete with his corporate mistress. So, she'd gotten out before she went from anger to hate. She didn't want to hate anyone, but she needed to be loved and wanted and fulfilled and Tate didn't have the time to give her that.

Maybe someday she'd find a man on the same wavelength she was, but she didn't have to wait around for him to start a family. She was thirty-three, and while that wasn't old, her chances of conceiving would begin to drop after thirty-five. Only two years away. If she waited and then couldn't have children, she'd regret it forever. Yes, she'd always imagined having Tate's children, but that wasn't going to happen and she had to move on. No more sitting around hoping her life would turn out the way she wanted. Time to make it happen. So, she had an appointment next month with a sperm bank. It had taken a lot of courage to make that appointment, another break from the life she thought she'd have. Her friends had already volunteered to go with her and help figure out which sperm donor to pick.

She really did have awesome friends.

After dinner, she sent the younger siblings back to their respective college campuses. Finn had gone off to return the rental truck and Lukas had followed in his car to bring the other man back. Which left Karen alone with her best friends.

Anne angled a glance at her. "Want us to do a sleepover for this first night?"

"We're totally willing," Julie quickly added. She pointed to Meg. "We already cleared it with the guys. Say the word, and Lukas will just drop Finn off at home instead of bringing him here."

Karen arched her eyebrows. "You don't have clothes with you."

"That wouldn't stop us." Meg shrugged, enough empathy in her gaze to make Karen's throat clog.

Moisture burned the backs of her eyes, and she had to blink fast to keep the tears from falling. No more crying. She'd done enough of that since she'd told her husband it was over. Sucking in a deep breath, she shook her head. "No, I think I need to rip the Band-Aid off and just do it."

It had been a decade since she'd slept alone in a house, except the handful of times Tate or she had gone out of town for work. She needed to get this over with, start to make this her routine. And it wasn't as if she'd be alone forever. If she were lucky, by this time next year, she'd have her hands full with a baby. Hard to feel alone when your roommate doesn't let you sleep through the night.

Julie shrugged. "I had a feeling you'd say that."

"Okay, but we're only a few minutes away if you need us for anything," Meg said.

"Seriously, Karen," Anne insisted. "Anything. A cup of sugar, company...borrowing from my extensive porn collection."

A round of groans spilled from the group.

"I'm just kidding! How would I have hidden a collection like that from the girls? They got into everything growing up." Anne ruffled a hand over her short red hair. "Besides, remember I live with the drama mama. You think I want her coming along to knock while I have that stuff playing?" She shuddered. "No thank you."

"She has a point." Karen had camped out on Anne's couch for the first few weeks after the break up, and she had gained a new appreciation for her friend's restraint in not killing her mother all these years. Karen was usually pretty even-tempered, but the drama llama mama could drive anyone to homicide.

Julie's nose wrinkled. "I don't even want to think about anyone but Lukas walking in on my lady time. I'm just saying. Gross."

"Finn likes watching my lady time." Meg flashed a wicked grin, even as a blush rushed up her cheeks.

A very juvenile round of hooting erupted from everyone, and Karen wanted to hug them. She wouldn't have gotten through this without them, certainly not without having a major mental breakdown. They made her laugh when all she'd wanted to do was cry. They'd helped her keep perspective.

"I love you guys." She looped her arms around Julie's and Anne's waists. Meg crowded in for a tangled group embrace. They held tight for a long time, and the support felt damn good—a bulwark of strength she could always depend on, that would see her through everything. Even divorce. "You guys really are the best, you know that, right?"

"'Course we know," Anne said gruffly, then ruined the tough act by giving a little sniffle. She pulled back and scrubbed a hand over her eyes.

Meg and Julie looked a bit teary too.

"Love you too." Meg went to grab a tissue. "We don't say it that often, but still. It's good to have you, even when you're being nosy and bossy."

"We're only nosy 'cause we care." Julie gave a lopsided grin, her eyes welling. "And I wouldn't have survived losing my Auntie Eloise without you girls. Thanks."

"Okay, let's pull it together or we'll scare the guys when they come back." Karen took a tissue Meg proffered and dabbed at her eyes. She pulled in a breath. "Let's meet for breakfast at the Moonside Café. I'll be okay on my own tonight."

"If you change your mind, the sleepover offer stands for tomorrow night or the night after." Anne waggled her eyebrows. "The porn offer already expired though."

"I think I'll survive the disappointment." Karen patted the redhead's shoulder.

A knock sounded on the door, then Finn poked his head in. His gaze lit on Meg and a smile spread across his lips. "Ready to go, honey?"

"Yeah."

He glanced at Julie. "Lukas couldn't find a parking space, so he's stuck in a red zone. He's waiting for you...if you're not having a girls' night." His eyebrows rose as he turned to Karen.

"Nope, they're all yours." Karen gave a magnanimous wave. "Thanks for all your help today."

He shrugged easily. "Any time. Happy to lend a hand."

An hour after they'd gone, Karen was still wandering around her apartment listlessly. She'd straightened pillows that didn't need it, checked cupboards that were neat and organized. Loneliness swamped her, which was ridiculous because if she were still living in their very expensive house in Palo Alto, Tate wouldn't even have been home from his law firm yet. His father would have insisted they stay longer, and Tate would have thrown himself into whatever case they were working on, and it would have been midnight before he crawled into bed beside his wife. She'd be lonely if she were there too. In the end, she thought that might have been what had done her in. Being in a marriage by yourself was a kind of hellish helplessness she wouldn't wish on her worst enemy.

Even this apartment's echoing aloneness was better. A sad, but true statement on her life.

For a moment, she considered calling Anne and asking her to come over. Unlike their other two friends, Anne was single and wouldn't have scheduled a date for tonight. Karen picked up her cell phone, her finger hovering over the speed dial that would connect her to the other woman.

No.

She stiffened her spine. This was the path she'd chosen and she needed to live with it. Alone. If that meant she'd spend the next two weeks crawling the walls between now and the start of her new job, then so be it. The antsy restlessness was annoying, but it would get better. It had to. Gritting her teeth, she moved to set the phone down when it blared out a ring.

Her heart leapt and her fingers clenched on the plastic so hard it squeaked. She pressed a hand to her chest and checked the screen to see who was calling. Brows arching in surprise, she smiled and accepted the call. "Valentina De Rossi, as I live and breathe."

"Karen, darling!" The other woman's musical Italian accent made Karen's name sound more exotic than it was. "I have the most wonderful news."

"Oh? Tell me." Karen smiled at Valentina's effusion. They'd met during Karen's junior year of college when she'd studied abroad in Rome, and had managed to become friends despite their wildly disparate personalities. Her smile faded. Unfortunately, that was also the year she'd met Tate, who'd been in Italy on foreign exchange too. Those lovely Roman memories she'd cherished had suddenly become a bit tarnished.

"Welllll," Valentina said, drawing the word out. "You know I've kept my Giovanni in suspense for quite some time."

"Only over a decade, but who's counting?"

In fact, Tate and Karen had been the ones to introduce Valentina to Giovanni. Another reminder she didn't want, but she shoved that away. It wasn't Gio or Valentina's fault that Karen was getting a divorce.

A tinkling laugh came through the phone. "I finally said yes! We're getting married next week."

"Next week?" Karen echoed.

"I know, it is rash and unplanned and exciting. Just as I like things. I was always so petrified of the huge wedding and all the planning and details that must be just so. And my mother and aunts and cousins...darling, you know how passionate the Italians are." She sighed dramatically. "There would be fighting. I didn't want the headache. But, my Gio, he knows me. He said I wouldn't be happy eloping because my family wouldn't be there, even though they drive me crazy. So he said our engagement will be very short—not enough time for huge planning or fighting. Just throw the kind of party I love with an even more beautiful and expensive dress."

Curling into the recliner in her living room, Karen grinned. "It was him offering you carte blanche on the expensive dress that convinced you, wasn't it?"

Valentina laughed. "It's entirely possible."

"He knows you so well," Karen murmured. She'd always liked Gio. He was every bit as passionate as Valentina, though with slightly less drama. Valentina was two handfuls, but he was stubborn enough to have hung on. Once he'd decided she was the one he wanted, that was the end of the discussion.

Karen hated to make comparisons between Gio and Tate on that score, but it was hard. Especially when she listened to her friend gush while she was sitting alone in an apartment because Tate had wanted everything else more than he'd wanted to keep her. For Gio, Valentina had always been the priority.

Karen shoved away the petty jealousy that wanted to consume her. No. What kind of friend would she be if she couldn't get past her own issues to be thrilled for two people who had always been genuinely kind to her? Gio and Valentina had come to visit several times over the years. Gio's investment firm had a branch in San Francisco, and he'd been sent on business trips which the couple had turned into vacations.

Valentina hesitated. "I know…things haven't been going so well for you lately." A graceful side step from mentioning the divorce. "But I had to share my happiness with someone who was there at the very beginning."

"I am happy for you. Both of you." And she was. Her own situation had nothing to do with theirs. "This is such good news."

Another small pause, and then Valentina's normal exuberance burst out. "Can you come? You must come. Please say you'll come."

Karen looked around her apartment, imagining how two weeks of sitting here by herself would feel. Like the walls were closing in on her. It wasn't as if she couldn't afford the trip. She hadn't spent a dime of her librarian salary in eight years, and even modest earnings added up after that much time. They'd lived off of Tate's income except the chunk of his trust fund they'd used to buy their house.

Besides, when was the last time she'd gone anywhere? Tate had always been too busy to go on vacation and she hadn't felt like going without him. So, she had two weeks off and a damn good reason to get out of town. She took a breath. "I'll come."

"Really?" The delight and disbelief that came through the line made Karen grin. She heard Valentina clap her hands. "*Magnifico!* Let me know when you'll arrive and I'll have Giovanni pick you up from the airport."

"I will. Thanks for thinking of me, Valentina."

"Of course, of course!"

Once they were off the phone, Karen punched the speed dial to connect to Anne.

She picked up on the first ring. "Need me to come over?"

"No, and I don't want your porn collection either." Karen propped her feet on the ottoman in front of her chair. "What I need is a ride to

SFO."